Hearts Unmasked

Ruth Madison

10% of net royalties from the sale of the Sledge Hockey Team Of Cedar Harbor series will be ***donated to https://www.bostonicestorm.org/*** *Boston's only sled hockey team founded and managed by people with disabilities.*

Titles In The Series

Thawing An Ice Heart

Saving His Soulmate

Hearts Unmasked

Love Comes Back

The Caring Heart

Chronically Yours

Contents

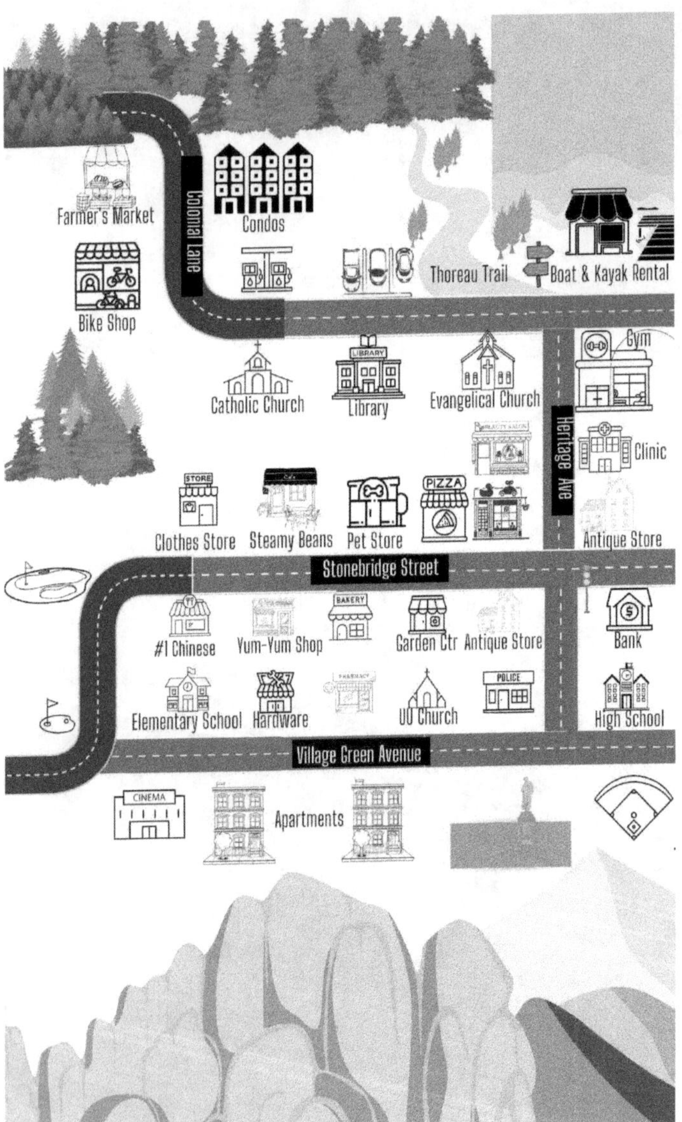

Colonial Lane
Farmer's Market
Condos
Bike Shop
Thoreau Trail
Boat & Kayak Rental
Gym
Catholic Church
Library
Evangelical Church
Heritage Ave
Clinic
STORE
PIZZA
Clothes Store
Steamy Beans
Pet Store
Antique Store
Stonebridge Street
BAKERY
#1 Chinese
Yum-Yum Shop
Garden Ctr
Antique Store
Bank
POLICE
Elementary School
Hardware
UU Church
High School
Village Green Avenue
CINEMA
Apartments

Cedar Harbor
Harbor View Road
Autumn Ridge Drive
Liquor Store
Historical Society
Veteran's Hall
Stop N Shop
Grocery
Synagogue
Middle School
Town Hall
Thatcher Memorial Rehab
Post Office
Cottage Grove Avenue
Red Barn Road
MOTEL
Phone Store
Daycare
The Whispering Pine
Cranberry Lane

Becca

Am I a bad person? What is bad or good when it comes to being a person anyway? My parents always told me there are no bad people, just bad actions and my observations so far have borne that out. I've never seen any bad behavior that I couldn't follow the thread back to fear. Scared people do scary things. But are they bad?

That's what I'm wondering as a gossip video plays on my TV and I knit a lace shawl for my sister's wedding veil. I wonder why I enjoy these videos gossiping about reality shows and does that enjoyment make me a bad person. My knitting needles continue to clack away as my mind goes deeper and deeper into this question. Luckily I have the lace pattern memorized by now.

What you enjoy watching must have some bearing on your moral character and I have no answer for why I find these stories of drama in the lives of people I don't know so interesting. I tell myself it's because I am an observer of human behavior, always trying to better understand how people connect to one another. But deep down my mind is skeptical of this explanation. Still, if I don't accept that explanation then the only other one I can think of is that it makes me a bad person to be enjoying it. I would rather not believe that. I'll have to keep observing.

One ball of cobweb thread finishes up and I have to get up to wind another skein to continue with the veil. This gift was my idea. It's an epic project made with the smallest of needles and thread. I hope that it expresses a form of love to my sister but who knows. She and I don't communicate well at all.

I'm not convinced that Leah actually wants me at her wedding but it would look strange if her own sister wasn't there so we have to do what's expected. Life would be nicer without the weight of those expectations. What if it were fine to admit that she doesn't particularly like me and not have it be a big deal?

I also don't think I'll enjoy the wedding much. I've never been to one but I understand there's a lot of people, loud music, crowded spaces, talking to people you don't know, and trying to look entertained by speeches. I shudder just thinking about it. Leah's going to make me be a bridesmaid too. Probably even maid of honor. She'll never agree to noise-canceling headphones so I'll have to wear earplugs and style my hair to cover them.

A funny commercial comes on the TV and I carefully lay down the knitting to pick up my notebook and write down the joke. I appreciate the juxtaposition of a serious person of power and authority doing something silly and mundane. Unexpected pairings like that can make great humor.

My phone alarm buzzes and it's nearly time for me to go over to my volunteer job at Thatcher memorial rehab center. I've given myself enough buffer that I have time to finish the row of knitting and fold it into my bag. Then I brush my thick wavy brown hair because my mother has told me never to leave the house without brushing it first. And even though I now live in an apartment and not a house, I do it anyway. I believe the intention of her statement was that no one outside see my hair in an unruly state. Brushing does not always accomplish that goal, however.

With my hair properly frizzed, I pick out a pair of my favorite socks. Once I found these socks I bought enough of them to get rid of all my other socks. The difference between these socks and the ones I used to have is subtle but when your senses don't process input correctly the right clothes help a lot. What I've learned over the years is that if I can do small things to avoid irritation it greatly reduces the chance of me having a meltdown. The little challenges and sensory processing issues build up until they reach explosion so if I can bring the stress levels back down in any way it prolongs the period of time I can spend out doing people things.

In my bag I have a light cardigan in case the air on my arms starts to bother me, ear plugs, a smooth stone that feels nice to stroke, a bottle of water and a snack bar. Before I leave my apartment I make sure it's all still packed in my bag and then I drive over to Thatcher.

I work from home so this volunteer job is one of the only things that gets me out of the house regularly, which is good for me. So my mother says.

Thatcher is a rehabilitation facility mostly for people with spinal cord injuries but they have patients learning to use wheelchairs for other reasons too.

I feel a kinship with the patients here even though I'm disabled in a very different way. However, I rarely talk to anyone. My job is to restock shelves, move chairs in and out of meeting rooms, fix little things. The staff do sometimes ask for my help with their computers because they know I work as a coder.

Just because I don't speak much doesn't mean I'm not listening so I hear all the gossip and drama about staff and about patients. Today one of the nurses is leaning over the reception desk and talking about a brand new patient whom she describes as handsome, rich, and annoying.

Most people come here still struggling to accept that their life has changed in ways they will never come back from but apparently, this guy is taking it to a whole new level. She says he's refusing to learn any wheelchair skills and is completely fixated on walking out of here healed. It can happen. It's not likely but it can happen. I say a silent little prayer to G-d in my head that this man finds peace either way.

Jack

I open my eyes and my brain scrambles to figure out what's going on. This is not my bed. This is not my bedroom. Despite the dim light I finally register that I'm in a hospital room. Then I remember the truck coming straight for my car across the turnpike the wrong way.

Thankfully I don't remember the impact. The last moment in my memory is thinking "Oh no" and then I woke up here.

I take inventory and realize the doctors must have put in a spinal block or an epidural or whatever because I can't feel anything below my waist. I almost laugh at what a cliche that phrase is. If this were a movie I'd really be in trouble.

I just need to wait for the medicine to wear off. Not a bad thing to get a few days rest and go back to work refreshed.

I try to close my eyes again but it's hard to get comfortable. There's an IV attached in my hand and low beeps every few moments from somewhere else in the room. And every time I close my eyes I see the truck coming at me and my upper body tenses anticipating the impact.

So instead I just rest the best I can. As my eyes adjust more I realize my mother is sleeping on a stiff recliner in the corner. Her eye makeup is streaked down her cheeks and the edge of her lipstick is no longer crisp. I must have given her a real scare.

Someone opens the door and immediately flicks on the light, flooding the room in bright fluorescence. Ouch. The light has woken my mother as well and she's slowly uncurling herself from the chair, staggering blearily to her feet.

"Jack, you're awake," the man who has the air of authority of a doctor says. "Excellent. If you'll allow me, I have a test for you.

"I'm great at tests," I say but my voice cracks and it comes out as a croak.

The doctor gives me a pity chuckle and raises a large metal tool that looks like a giant needle. My mother is standing to his side with her arms crossed over her chest. She hasn't said anything and her face is as serious as I've ever seen it.

Lifting the thin blanket off my legs, the doctor pokes at them. "Do you feel this?" he asks.

"No, whatever you gave me hasn't worn off."

To my surprise, my mother makes a strangled sort of sound in her throat.

The doctor sighs a little. Asks a few more times if I can feel him poking. When he makes it up to my belly button I feel it but it's a much duller sensation than the tip of the needle would suggest.

"Look Jack, you've suffered a severe spinal cord injury from the accident."

Sluggishly my brain tries to process what that means.

He continues, "This is one of the few areas of medicine where we still have a lot of work to do. I've done what I can for your spine but I have to let you know that you have a complete severing of your spinal cord and it's very likely that you'll be in a wheelchair for the rest of your life. I don't want to discourage you but I also don't want to give you false hope. The plain and simple data shows that your odds for regaining control of your lower body are very slight."

I blink at him. I'm barely registering what he's saying. For a moment I think of old Peanuts cartoons and the garbled nonsense the adults are always saying.

"Jack," my mother says, stepping closer until I can smell her lilac and rose perfume. "Do you understand what the doctor is saying?"

I do understand. He's issued a challenge. I know my role in this story and that is to overcome. Beating the odds is what great men do and I was raised to be great. If anyone can defy the odds it's me.

I can see exactly how my story will be told. I will make a triumphant return to the bank as the man who overcame a devastating accident. This chapter will fade into the past as an interesting experience I once had that helped me grow stronger as an individual. I know how to work hard and I'll work harder at recovery than I've ever worked at anything. It's all going to be fine.

"I'll give you some time to process that," the doctor says and leaves the room as suddenly as he came.

I look at my mother, her face pale in the bright light. “I remember a truck,” I say.

She picks up the thread of the conversation. “I spoke to the police at the scene. It seems the truck driver suffered a heart attack while on the road, lost control of the vehicle. He died on the scene.”

While I take that in she says, “I’m going to go let everyone know you’re awake.” By everyone she means my father, my two brothers, and my sister. I’m not sure I’m ready to see all of them and try to explain the challenge facing me.

I’m angry at the truck driver for dying. Angry at him for having a heart attack. He couldn’t help it but what do I do without someone to blame?

I’m not going to let this ruin my life, I reiterate to myself. This is going to be just a blip and I’ll have an inspiring story to share when I get back to my real life.

When my mother returns I ask, “Where’s my phone? I need to talk to work.”

“It was broken in the accident,” she says. “I’ve ordered a new one but it hasn’t arrived yet.”

Fuck. This day just keeps getting better.

My work is fast-moving and high-pressure. Decisions have to be made constantly and quickly.

"Let me see yours," I say and she hands over her rose gold iPhone. My arms are sore and my fingers fumble with it but I manage to leave a voicemail for my direct supervisor. I'll need to get hold of a computer with WiFi soon to keep up with stock market trends but I'll try to take this opportunity for a little break.

In fact, I'm quite tired. My brain is trying to process a lot right now. I don't usually sleep much but right now I can't keep my eyes open any longer.

The next time I wake up it again takes me a moment to remember where I am and what's going on. My throat is parched and I fumble to find the button to call a nurse. A voice comes over a speaker somewhere and I request a water.

I wonder if I need to pee. With whatever is blocking my feeling below the waist I have no idea. Then I see the tube on the side of the bed and realize there's a catheter in my dick. This is whole new levels of absurd. The last time I was overnight at a hospital was the day I was born. I've been healthy and lucky my entire life.

The nurse comes in with a thin plastic cup of cold water and ice cubes like you get at a restaurant. I gulp it down in seconds.

I hear my father's voice long before he reaches the doorway. He has that booming way about him.

"There he is!" My father says as he enters the room. As usual his clothes are immaculate and a glint of gold cufflink shines in the fluorescent light. He puts my laptop and a new phone down on the table beside the bed. "Your mother said you were looking for these."

"Thanks, Dad."

He smiles and pats my shoulder. "Not going to let a little set back like this slow you down, are you?"

"Not a chance," I say.

His phone rings and he's off again but I've got what I wanted, the laptop and phone. I'm anxious to check in with work.

I call Tom's extension and this time he picks up. "I heard your voicemail, are you all right? What's going on?"

At this point there isn't really an answer to that question. "I'm all right but I'm going to be stuck here at the hospital for a bit. I've got my laptop so I'm going to get started on the quarterly audit for the trust accounts."

"Are you sure? You should focus on healing."

"I've got it. But there are some in-person things I won't be able to do. You'll need to set up a meeting with the Carlisle Foundation to finalize account details."

"Will do."

"Awesome. I'll check in again tomorrow. Send a text if you need anything."

I'm sure in theory my job can't fire me for time spent recovering from an injury but I know they would find a way. Millions of dollars are hanging in the balance every day. If I take a break the industry will leave me in the dust.

I raise the back of my bed with a button and put my laptop on a tray. First thing to do is change all my Zoom meetings to phone instead. I don't want any of my clients seeing me in this state.

An hour later I'm going over pro formas with a client. A nurse comes in to take my vitals and I try to shoo her away but she's not having it. I keep talking until she sticks a thermometer in my mouth.

After that call I turn to profit and loss statements. December is probably the worst time for me to get laid up. The final quarter of the year is wrapping up and it's the busiest time. My back is aching. I adjust my pillows and try to find a position that puts less pressure on my spine but it's not working.

Dear God, I hope this is all over with soon.

Becca

Almost all my life I've been told that my brain is different. Different from what, I'm not sure. The impression I've been given is that the majority of people all think in very similar ways and I'm thinking in entirely different ways.

While there are times people look at me like they have no idea how I've gotten to the conclusion I have or tell me that I'm not having the correct (or as they say "human") reaction to something, I can't really believe that brains are wired vastly differently.

If only I could know what it looks like inside other people's brains. If I could ever make a genie wish it would be to know how other people's brains think. Maybe mine is slightly different from the norm. Maybe each and every one of us has a different brain and someone decided to draw a line and say, these brains are autistic and these other ones are normal.

Although if the reality TV shows I watch are actually reflecting reality then there are people who are seeing the world extremely differently from me.

After my shift at Thatcher I leave my car in the lot and walk over to the grocery store where my best friend Sam works. Sam is short for Samantha but she introduced herself to me as Sam at summer camp when we were thirteen so I can't attach any other name to her.

Sam is great at helping me with my self-improvement list. She gets me in a way that almost no one else does. Being around her isn't a strain like it is with most people. I don't have to second guess what I say or put energy into worrying that I've done something wrong. Around her I can just relax and be myself. It's quite a relief.

My self-improvement list is in my notebook that I always carry in my bag. I believe in making myself a better person and always striving to conquer new challenges. Last month Sam started helping me with small talk. I'll admit I still have a ways to go on that one.

As I walk into the grocery store I'm relieved to see that Sam is at the customer service desk. Even though she has a set schedule (which I have memorized), they send her to different tasks in the store each time. The grocery store is already overwhelming and when I'm not sure where to go to find Sam it can send me into a terrible spiral.

So much of my life is about managing my environment. In my quest for self-improvement I used to always push myself out of my comfort zone and chastise myself for the meltdowns that would inevitably follow. There have been positives to that approach. I used to not be able to go into grocery stores at all.

I would freeze in the doorway and feel myself instantly filling up with all the sensory input like a container being filled too quickly, overflowing almost immediately. I practiced and did baby steps with Sam's help and now I can actually spend significant time in the store hanging out with her.

However, now that I'm a little older I try to respect my limits and not push as hard as I used to. I can still make progress without putting my mind and body under so much stress. I realize now that managing my environment and making careful decisions about what I take on allows me to do a lot more.

Sam smiles as she sees me walk up. It's such a relief to have her back. She disappeared last month and scared me so badly. Now her evil ex-husband is in jail, at least for a little while. He basically kidnapped her in her own home. That man is a data point in favor of there being actually bad people in this world. I shiver and pull the light cardigan out of my bag. It's not so much for cold as it is because the sensation of air on the skin of my arms can irritate me. Things are back to normal now with Sam. Better than normal, even, since Sam has a new beaux and I like him much better.

"What's on the list today?" she asks me.

"Eye contact," I say. Classic autism problem. It's very intense looking into people's eyes. For a long time I've been getting by with looking at the bridge of people's noses but I'm not sure if I'm actually fooling anyone.

"Hmmmm. I don't think about how I do eye contact," Sam says. She turns her attention away as a customer walks up and I watch while Sam goes over her receipt with her but then her attention comes back immediately to me and she picks up the thread of her thought without interruption. "Eye contact is mostly to show that you are interested and paying attention. If you're looking at something else people will think you aren't listening to them. It can be brief. Maybe just look long enough to see what color their eyes are?"

"That's a good idea." I make a note in my notebook. When I look back up Sam is smiling at me.

"Look how far you've come," she says. "I remember when you couldn't even walk through the doors of the store."

"Me too." That's the thing about self-improvement. It's not just to fit in better with people around me, it's also for me to live a fuller life, less hemmed in by limitations. I suppose that's the main thing that makes autism a disability for me. I'm lucky, I've been told many times that I have what they call fewer support needs. I'm smart, I'm verbal, I can care for myself. Not everyone with autism can say the same.

Sometimes I wonder if my diagnosis was correct. There's people with so much more severe symptoms and it's hard to look at someone with what they call "higher support needs" and dare to think that I have what they have.

There's a lot of fighting in the autism community about the language that we use. High functioning is out of favor. But that's how I see myself. And when I look at people with more obvious symptoms it's not that I'm looking down on them in any way, but it seems disrespectful to their struggles to say that I have the same diagnosis. Okay it's not exactly the same, there are levels of autism. As they say, it's a spectrum and it's a very long spectrum.

I'm lucky because I can live independently and I can communicate well. Some of that has been practice. I used to have a harder time talking and for a while I wrote everything instead but now I rarely find it hard to speak.

In some ways I fool myself into believing that I'm doing better simply because I do so much to control my environment and prevent it from triggering issues for me.

"You're coming to dinner with me and Rob tomorrow night, right?"

"Wouldn't miss it." They always make me feel included and not like a third wheel. With all the volunteer work I do around wheelchairs that expression is really odd. Nothing balances with just two wheels, does it? Fifth wheel would make more sense. Then it's actually unnecessary.

Sam and I chat for a while longer and then it's time for me to go back home for work. I walk back to my car, stepping carefully through a light dusting of snow.

I honestly hate driving but I hate public transit more. As stressful as driving is, waiting for a bus and being surrounded by strangers is much worse. The first time I tried to use a bus I didn't know how you were supposed to ask it to stop or how to tell where my stop was. I panicked and had a meltdown.

I absolutely hate having meltdowns. That may be obvious but it's more than just how scary it is for me, it's also humiliating when it happens in public. I'm aware of people staring at me in horror but I'm powerless to do anything about it. I lose all ability to control my distress and collapse on the ground shrieking and I literally can't help it. It's horrible.

And often I end up hurting myself as well. The lead up to a meltdown has me desperately trying to manage the stress to prevent it spilling over and that usually involves pinching myself, biting myself, hitting my face, or scratching myself. There's a tiny scar on my hand where I picked my skin while my mom berated me for forgetting to open my mail for a month and missing a car insurance payment. I might have executive dysfunction but I've got to do better to function as an adult.

At home I instantly relax as I walk in the door. It's like slipping out of a coat or taking off a bra to finally be alone in my own space. No more stress of managing how other people are responding to me.

It's time for work and I load up my computer.

I should probably eat something but the thought is exhausting. I don't know what to eat and I don't have the motivation to put any effort into making something. This is why I have boxes of protein bars. As long as I actually remember to eat them. I try to build it into my routine so I've taught myself to think of eating whenever I open the door to my apartment.

I grab one bar and sit down to immerse myself in coding. The main thing I do is locate the errors in other people's code. I can hunt down the place where something is going wrong and preventing the whole code from producing the right results. They call it bug hunting, which makes me laugh. I love telling people that my job is bug hunting.

Since coders can be sensitive about their mistakes I have a direct manager who is the go-between. I tell him the fixes and he says whatever magic words the engineers need to hear to not get upset about changes. Basically I have the perfect job and I love it. I sit at my computer and dig so deep into code that hours fly by and I feel energized by it.

Often I set an alarm to remind me to stop and go to bed.

I enjoy the work so much that I never think of keeping track of actually getting paid for it. After a few disasters now my dad monitors my bank account to make sure that my paychecks come in. It's a relief not to have to check on that.

Before bed I do some more knitting. I set an alarm to remind me to stop but to be honest I don't always listen to it. Once I start doing something I don't like to have to stop. Tonight I nod off with the gossamer thread piled on my legs and the sharp little knitting needles clutched in my hands. Some time in the middle of the night I wake up enough to put them down on the floor.

The next evening I meet up with Robbie and Sam at #1 Chinese in Cedar Harbor at the end of Stonebridge Street.

When I arrive they're already there. Sam is in a booth and Robbie's wheelchair is sticking out at the end of the table. The space is pretty limited in here. They don't have any regular tables. I slide into the other side of the booth.

"Hey, Becca," Robbie says. "How is Thatcher doing without me?"

He likes to say that even though he finished his rehab years ago. "You were there for basketball practice three days ago," I point out.

"I live in the present," he says with a wink.

Sam hands me the menu but I already know I'm just going to get dumplings. It's not that I want to have such a limited palette but expanding my food horizons is further along in my self-improvement list.

Robbie and Sam talk about what they are going to share. When you see them together you just know that true love exists. It's inspiring, honestly.

"Are you looking forward to Leah's wedding?" Sam asks me.

I sigh. "Um, I'm sure I'll get through it."

"Your bridesmaid's dress is really pretty."

"Thank you. I didn't pick it out, of course, but I do like what she chose."

"Do you have a date?" Robbie asks.

"If my mother has her way I'll be going with Paul Abelman." I can't help but make a face.

"That good, huh?" Robbie says.

Sam laughs. "You don't need him," she says to me. "Better to be alone than with the wrong person."

"Is Paul the wrong person?" Robbie asks.

Sam shrugs. "I'm sure he's fine but he's boring and he certainly doesn't light Becca up."

"True," he says nodding.

Robbie is deeply kind. You can feel it in everything he does. He doesn't have to think about it, it just is. In fact, I envy Robbie's ability to just do things without getting trapped in endless loops of thought.

The food arrives and while I eat my dumplings I watch Robbie and Sam laughing as he tries to get food to his mouth when his fingers don't work. I know he's got special silverware to strap onto his hands but he doesn't seem to be bothered by doing it the challenging way. He's very at peace with himself and his body.

When he was first injured as a teenager of course it was a tough adjustment, it always is. But he has grown into one of the most confident and content people I've ever met.

We end the evening with ice cream cones from the Yum Yum Shop next door. Sam holds Robbie's cone for him and it's just the cutest thing you've ever seen.

Leah and Larry don't act like this but it's her life and you never know what's going on in other people's relationships really.

Jack

Even though I'm finished at the hospital they won't let me go home yet. Instead I'm transferred over to Thatcher Memorial Rehab in Cedar Harbor so I can keep working on recovery. It's a daunting task coming back from an injury like this but I have confidence in myself. They load me onto a short bus with a wheelchair lift and strap down the wheelchair I'm in for the drive to Cedar Harbor.

I've been there before. Dated a girl once who lives there. I've gone to charity galas to support Thatcher, in fact. And here I am being shuttled over on a short bus. Even the beautiful New England fir trees weighted down with snow that I can see through the window can't dispel my funk. I can't wait for this chapter of my life to be over.

At the rehab facility they push me to a room and lift me up onto the bed. At this point I can literally do almost nothing for myself but I keep being reassured that will change here at Thatcher. They say a cheerful goodbye and take the wheelchair with them. It was just on loan from the hospital. I'm sure they must have a similar program here.

I've got my laptop bag so I take the opportunity to dive back into work. I'm thankful that my mother brought me some of my clothes too so instead of sweats I'm wearing a green polo shirt and slacks.

There's a light rap on the open door and I look up to see a short wiry Black woman in a white coat. She's nearly vibrating with energy.

"I'm Dr. Wilson," she says. "I'm the head doctor at Thatcher and I wanted to personally welcome you and explain a little about our program."

I'm too polite to glower at her so I say nothing and let her tell me about therapy sessions, meal times, events, and the like. When she says physical therapy is two hours in the morning and an hour in the afternoon I finally speak up. "I can do more if I want to, right?"

She pauses a moment. "You can," she says. "But this program has been designed by professionals to make sure you reach important milestones without burnout or further injury."

Probably professionals who have never been in my position.

Before she leaves Dr. Wilson says, "Your first physical therapy session will be here in your room in twenty minutes. After that is group therapy in the main hall. It's mandatory."

I'm a grown-ass man and they want to tell me what to do every second of every day. I hate it here already. But that just means I have to work extra hard to get better and back to my real life.

A little while later a friendly-looking young man appears in the doorway. "Hi, Jack," he says. "I'm Bill and I'm your physical therapist."

"Good to meet you," I say. That part is true. I am eager to get started in recovering physically.

"For this first session I just want us to get to know each other and do some simple exercises to see where we're starting from," Bill says.

Ugh. Let's get this over with so I can start actually beating the odds and proving the doctors wrong. I put the laptop aside.

So far I haven't gained any more sensation. My legs feel like when you've slept funny and your limbs have gone to sleep so completely you can't feel them at all. I keep anticipating that painful pins and needles as the blood flow returns but it never comes.

I use my arms to push up against the bed but they have gotten weak and the blood rushes out of my head making me dizzy. Bill is not surprised and he holds me steady until my head stops swimming. He has me do simple things like push against his hands and before I know it the twenty minutes is up.

"Let's get you over to group therapy," Bill says. He goes out and comes back a moment later with a wheelchair.

The last thing I want to do is group therapy. I don't want to listen to people whine about their lot in life and I sure as hell don't want to talk about myself and my feelings about this nightmare.

"I'm going to help you get in and in our next session we'll start building the skills for you to transfer into the wheelchair yourself. After therapy a nurse will come to get you back into bed, okay?"

What would happen if I said no it's not okay? I think the choice is an illusion right now. Bill gets his arms under me and lifts me like a goddamn baby. He places me down on the chair and puts each of my feet onto a metal plate. The chair practically swallows me up. I've lost a lot of weight in the last few weeks.

"I'll get you over to the main hall and if you need help getting back just let the therapist know and she'll get someone, okay?"

He likes to couch everything he says with that illusion of choice.

Bill pushes me out of the room and down a few hallways. The building is sleek and bright with gleaming white walls and many windows. I catch sight of myself in a mirror and my first thought is I need to get a barber in. I'm looking scruffy. We arrive at a wide open door with a plaque that says Main Hall. Inside is a large room with a couple tables along one wall and a few folding chairs but most of the people are in wheelchairs like the one I'm in. There's a couple of women but it's almost all men.

Bill leaves me there and reminds me that I can ask for help any time. Yeah I'll be avoiding that the best I can. I try pushing the wheels myself and it's not bad. If only my arms hadn't lost so much muscle tone.

Once the therapist arrives we all end up in a circle and it feels like an AA meeting in the worst possible way. I mostly try to tune it out as everyone tells their story of how they were injured. When the therapist gets to me I shake my head and she moves on. Someday I'll tell my story, when it's in the past.

***

Over the next several days I spend every waking hour I can in the therapy room. There are parallel bars, which is my main focus. Bill will strap braces onto my legs then I can heave myself up and practice walking.

It's not really walking, honestly. My legs and feet are still being stubborn and I don't have any ability to move them so it's really me pulling them along with my core muscles as I grip the two bars.

"Can we work on some wheelchair skills after you do the parallel bars?" Bill asks.

I reach the end of the bars and collapse back onto the wheelchair, sweat dripping down the back of my neck. "No," I say.

"Everyone fights it at first," Bill says with a shrug. He doesn't understand. I'm not like everyone else. I am in control of my destiny and I am not going to let this define me.

"People recover from these things all the time. You see it on the news," I say. I rub the back of my hand across my forehead and Bill hands me a bottle of water. Drinking it reminds me that I still haven't regained control of my bladder either. That's probably the worst part of all of this. The nurses put a catheter in and at least I can't feel it.

Bill says, "Recovering from a spinal cord injury depends mostly on the kind of injury. You've got a complete injury. It's good to push yourself and work hard but the truth is that in the first year is when you'll gain back as much function as you'll ever have. Even if you don't get function back, there's no limit to the skills you can master to live life on your terms."

I don't respond to that. "Let's get back to it," I say, reaching for the parallel bars again and pulling my body up to standing. If one year is the count down then I still have months left to get into shape.

***

I'm trying not to let my work suffer as I spend so much time in physical therapy. I'm determined to do both and failure is simply not an option.

While I'm on the phone my mother slips into the room and waits quietly for me to finish the call.

"I brought you your necessities." She hands me a week-ender tote bag and I can see she's packed my electric razor, my skin care kit, my cologne, a few pairs of pressed khaki pants and some polo shirts. Even my favorite loafers. And of course my electric toothbrush, floss, toothpaste, and mouthwash. I'll be feeling like myself again in no time.

"Thanks, mom."

She's not comfortable with praise or gratitude or emotions of any kind really so she changes the subject immediately. "I'm staying at the most delightful little B&B so I can be close to you through all of this. You should come and see it sometime. The ladies who run it are a hoot."

My mother must be feeling better about the whole situation since she's more chipper than I've seen her since the accident. I'm not sure about the staying nearby, though. I'm not used to having her or any of my family up in my business like this.

"How is work going?" she asks.

I consider carefully how to answer that. I'm starting to get the questions every day of when do I expect to be back at the office.

Even though all the banks I work at are accessible I can't imagine myself showing up to work in a wheelchair.

At this point the wheelchair sales people have been through several times. It turns out I'm expected to get measured and place an order for a long term chair. The ones I've been using are big, clunky, and hard to use. They aren't meant for taking home with you. But I keep sending the people away. I don't intend to take any wheelchair home with me. I don't care that I can customize the color of the spokes or put light-up caster wheels on it. I'm not twelve.

Tom has asked me to dial back and take time to recover. I'm afraid it's just the first step in distancing me from my work and making it easier to phase me out. He might be starting to catch on that this is not going to be a simple recovery situation. I can't relinquish any of my work or I might never be able to get back into it.

Finally I just say, "It's great."

At the group therapy meetings I'm still not saying much.

"Today let's talk about identity," Dr. Julia starts. "What are some of the things that you've typically attached your identity to? Work? Hobbies?"

She raises her eyebrows at one guy indicating for him to answer first. He's a young guy wearing jeans and a Red Sox cap. He's got his custom-fitted wheelchair unlike me still using the creaky old metal junk heap. In most things I take great care with my appearance but I refuse to see the wheelchair as an extension of myself.

The young guy says, "I'm an artist. I'm supposed to be starting a tattoo apprenticeship."

"How do your friends see you?" Dr. Julia asks.

A tiny smile tugs at the side of his mouth. "The life of the party," he says. "Always up for an adventure."

"Do any of those identities need to shift or change now that you're adding a disability identity?"

"I don't know. I guess not," he says and he seems pleased.

"Up for the new adventure?" Dr. Julia says with a warm smile and he nods.

"What about you?" She turns to a woman. "What identities do you connect to?"

"I'm a mom. I have four kids. They need me to take care of them. I can't be the one being cared for. How can I be the mom I want to be now?"

"There's many moms who have disabilities. I'll connect you with a lovely woman who became a mom after she was paralyzed. She can give you some good tips. Her kids are growing up with a lot of empathy and care for others."

Dr. Julia looks at me but I look down at my slacks. With all the exercising I'm doing, I haven't lost muscle tone in my legs. In fact, I have more now than I did when I arrived since the time at the hospital wasted me away a bit. My legs look healthy and fine except for how unmoving they are.

I'm still waiting to feel those painful pins and needles that will signal them waking up.

I don't want to open up and talk with these people. I don't relate to them and I don't feel like we have anything in common. What the hell is a disability identity?

More people talk about how they can integrate disability into their vision of themselves. I don't want to do that. All I've ever heard all my life is that I am in control of my destiny and I can create my reality. I am not going to accept a reality in which I'm disabled.

These group therapy sessions aren't helping me with my actual goals. I'd rather be spending the time in the physical therapy room but I'm already doing two to three times more physio than anyone else here.

After the session I hang around unsure what to do with myself next. I was supposed to have a meeting but it got canceled last minute. I sit to the side and listen as one guy tells another one a joke.

“I bet I can get you to say the word ‘blue’,” the first guy says.

“Deal,” says the second one.

“What color is the sky?”

“Aqua.”

“What color is the grass?”

“Green.”

“What color is my shirt?”

“Teal.”

“Gotcha!”

“What?! I didn’t say blue!”

The first guy starts laughing uproariously, holding onto the seat of his wheelchair. “Now you have,” he says. The two guys head out, wheeling side by side.

Ridiculous.

A female voice nearby says, “With jokes like that you have to stay vigilant because they trick you into thinking the game is over and then you relax. That’s the key to making it work.”

I look over and there’s a small young woman with curly brown hair putting out paper cups on a table at the far side of the room.

"Did you just analyze that joke?" I ask.

"Of course. I got tired of missing the joke all the time so I set out to learn what was funny. And I succeeded."

I don't even know what to say to that but there's something so oddly charming about her pride for such a strange thing.

"I'm Jack," I say.

"Becca," she replies. She doesn't stop setting up the table so I wheel my way over there. She doesn't seem to feel any pressure to keep the conversation going, she just continues to set up.

I know I can come across as sour and I'm not the best person in the world. Probably my best quality, though, is how much I enjoy listening to people talk about things they're passionate about. I learn so much and the way people light up when they explain things they love is beautiful.

"Tell me more," I say. "What have you learned about jokes?"

"You really want to know?" She's giving me a very skeptical look.

I chuckle. "I promise that I do."

"Well the most important part of most humor is the misdirection. You set something up and then subvert the expectations of what you'll say next. But the key is that the follow up has to still answer the set up. Unless you're going for absurdist but that's harder to pull off. And there's so many different types of jokes. Like sometimes it's about observing everyday situations so closely that you hone in on unexpected details. Or you manage to capture the thoughts we have about a situation that are nearly subconscious. We don't call them out within ourselves but then someone else does and we are startled by how well they captured it. And usually the thought is some part of the ordinary every day that is absurd when you look at it closely. Most jokes need tension where you build up an expectation or a curiosity, then pause, and deliver the surprise. That's probably why I'll never be funny. Not intentionally anyway. Many people are uncomfortable with tension but I can't stand it at all. That's why I can't really lie. I mean I could but it's painful. The tension of misleading someone wants to resolve itself as quickly as possible. I think that's why I'm so literal too. Because misdirection and being misleading is so uncomfortable for me that I forget other people don't have as hard a time with it. And being non-literal is a kind of mis-direction in some ways of looking at it."

"That's fascinating."

"Sorry, I talk too much."

I can see why people may have told her that and it breaks my heart a little that she has come to mistrust people enjoying what she has to say. "You don't talk too much," I say. "I just learned a whole lot."

"I'm autistic," she says out of the blue. "I've found that it's best to tell people that right away."

"What makes you think you need to give new people that head's up?"

"Past experience."

"How so? How have people responded to you?"

"When people are being kind they call me quirky or eccentric. Sometimes behind my back I find out they're calling me weird, dense, and socially awkward. My sister says I use autism as an excuse to be rude but that's not what I'm intending to do. I tell people not for an excuse but so they aren't confused or surprised if I misread a situation or say the wrong thing. If I don't do it then I tend to upset and offend people. When they understand that I'm seeing things from a different perspective they have more patience with me."

"You don't seem rude," I say.

She eyes me a moment and then says, "Maybe not yet, anyway."

I have to laugh but Becca just looks sad.

"I don't know anything about autism," I admit. "You'll have to be the example for me."

"That's too much responsibility," she protests.

"Then just tell me how do you find autism impacts your life the most?"

"No one has ever asked me that before."

"I like learning about people." And while I'm focused on her I can ignore the strange sensation of sitting but not feeling my butt beneath me. I'm already sick to death of thinking about myself, worrying about my body and my future.

"I guess the main thing is my sensory issues. Apparently my body overreacts to a lot of different kinds of sensory input. I don't know what it feels like to be anyone other than me but I often find that noises are too loud to deal with, lights are too bright, and it's especially bad with textures. Like I can't stand the feel of silk."

I think of my extensive collection of silk ties. I can't imagine. I love the unique sheen of silk thread.

"And food," she continues. "I'm pretty limited in what I can eat because of the intense textures and flavors."

"I'm pretty picky myself," I say, "And I don't have an excuse for it."

She smiles. She has a cherubic face and her smile brightens my mood like a light shining into my soul.

"Do you mind?" she asks and I see that she's finished with the table. Now she's sat down and pulled out what I think is knitting.

"What are you making?" I ask.

"It's a veil for my sister's wedding," she says.

"That sounds ambitious," I say.

"I suppose it is."

"My sister is getting married too," I say. "Is yours older or younger?"

"Older."

"Mine is younger."

I really should get back to my room and load up my laptop to get back to work but it would be nice to have a friend here. Becca is a fascinating character. I never quite know what she's going to say next. Keeps me on my toes, as the expression goes. And okay yes she's also beautiful. Despite my WASP upbringing I've always been drawn to Jewish women.

So instead of working I stay and talk with her more.

The next time I run into Becca she's crouched in a supply closet. I wheel up behind her and say, "Why did the chicken cross the road?"

She turns around and says, "You know, other autistic people have tried to claim 'getting to the other side' means getting hit by a car and dying. They say we are taking it too literally and it's meant to have this other layer of meaning. But I think what makes it funny is that your brain is trying to come up with a meaningful answer when the actual answer is absurdly simple. What do you think?"

"I think you're the expert on jokes."

She smiles. "I'm practicing eye contact, how is it?"

"Creepy."

"Oh." Her face falls and then I feel bad.

"Just trying to joke," I say. "Subvert your expectations."

"Really?"

"Sure."

"You must tell me the truth so I can keep improving."

"You're doing great."

After that I start seeing Becca all over the place. And each time I see her I ask her to tell me a joke and she giggles. She may not think she's funny but she's the most unintentionally funny person I've ever met.

Between keeping up with work, doing all the physio and then some, and the mandatory therapy, I'm busier here in rehab than I've ever been. And that's saying something because my work keeps me extremely busy.

Yet I start finding time to hang out with Becca. She is so completely without guile that is a refreshing change from the societal machinations that I'm used to.

Becca

I think sleep is the strangest thing in the world and no one talks about how weird it is. We sort-of turn off our consciousness. Things can be happening around you when you're asleep and you have absolutely no idea. But the consciousness is doing something. Dreaming, making fantastical stories. Why? And why does every single animal of every kind do it?

Plus, people say that you can pinch yourself in your dream to know if you're dreaming but that's not even true. I've tried it. Once I had a dream where I told Sam that I know it's not a dream because I can use all five of my senses and if I were dreaming I wouldn't be able to do that. I demonstrated. But it was actually still a dream. That's wild. Why are we not talking about that? How are we so many years into research and study and still no one is sure why we sleep?

Don't get me started on thinking. I wish I knew how chemicals firing in the brain created complex thoughts and pondering like this.

I'm driving down to Connecticut for Hanukkah with my family. It's not a huge deal for us. We do a bigger event for Passover. But it's a nice excuse to go back home.

When I'm driving my mind really goes down these rabbit holes wondering about the nature of life.

I arrive at my childhood home just before dinner time and let myself in the front door. It's a relatively grand house. A little white dog named Moose skitters over the tile to jump and lick at my knees. I sit down on the floor and he tries to sit in my lap but he's too excited and his butt keeps bouncing back up. I laugh and scratch him behind the ear.

I can hear voices in the kitchen and after a moment my dad pops around the corner. "There you are," he says and I stand to embrace him. He gives me a squeeze and asks how the trip was. Classic dad.

We walk together back to the kitchen where my mother and Leah are preparing dinner and gossiping. Leah's fiance is sitting at the table reading on his phone.

I don't know why but I suddenly wonder what it would be like if Jack were here. I've been spending a lot of time with him and it's strange but I miss him already. Like Sam, he's someone who lets me just be myself and it feels so nice to be around him. I can actually picture him sitting at that table next to Larry and the two of them talking about finance stuff.

It's dumb to think about that. I've always been told that no one will want to be with me like that long-term. I annoy people, I bore them, I'm too much to take. I get attached to people when they actually listen to me and give me some attention. It's not the first time I've developed a crush on a man just because he let me talk about my interests. And Jack is the sort of guy who would never go for me anyway. Everything about him is crisp and perfect while I am pure chaos.

"Don't just stand there," my mother says. "Set the table."

I wash my hands and pull out the white and blue plates.

I'm having feelings. I'm not sure what the feelings are but they are definitely there. One of the most frustrating things in my life is not being able to track down the source of a feeling. In my work I can hunt down errors in code and resolve them. In my real life I don't know how to hunt down the source of a feeling or even what that feeling is. I just know the symptoms.

Right now something deep within feels just a little bit off like I need to realign a toy train on a wooden track. But I don't know how, which is very frustrating.

Once everyone starts eating I like to watch the others as they put the food into their mouths. It's weirdly satisfying and I've found that I can sometimes even feel sated just from watching someone else eating. There's something psychological in that. I wonder if other people have noticed that and if it's been studied at all. You would think that watching other people eat would make you more hungry and give you a desire for food yet my observation has been the opposite of that. And while I struggle with the varied textures and mixtures of food from a sensory perspective, seeing all the different colors and shapes going into someone else's mouth is beautiful.

Leah snaps her fingers in front of my face and I startle. "What are you even thinking about?" she says.

"I was just wondering how much our brains attempt to sync up with each other. Like how I can imagine the taste of the food that you're eating."

Leah rolls her eyes. "You think you're so deep, don't you?"

"Not particularly." Does she not wonder about things like that?

Larry says, "Not like other girls, eh?"

I mean, I'm a lot like plenty of other girls. All of them autistic.

After dinner we light the menorah candles together. The rituals of Judaism are very comforting to me.

Each step anchors something in the physical world to something in the spiritual world, knitting them together into one cloth.

"How is Samantha doing?" My mother asks. She has a soft spot in her heart for my best friend because Sam stayed with us for a while when she escaped from the cult she grew up in. She's still estranged from her biological family so we've become her family in most ways. I didn't tell Mom about Sam's abusive husband trying to kidnap her because I didn't want Mom to worry. But she does know about the divorce.

"She's great. The divorce is final and she's been seeing a very nice boy that I know from when he went through the rehab program at Thatcher." I know everyone who has done their rehab at Thatcher for the last twelve years.

"So he's handicapped?"

"He's quadriplegic but it's low level and he's very independent. You'll like him. His name's Robbie."

As we talk I've got my knitting out. Dad is watching football on the TV while Leah and Larry are in a heated discussion over seating charts for the wedding, their heads together, furious whispering coming from that corner of the room.

It doesn't escape my notice that I'm the only one without a partner. I always try to tell myself that I'm fine on my own.

Other people just cause complications. But in moments like this I would like to have someone who is all mine and here just for me.

"Tell Samantha to come for Passover and she can bring her boyfriend."

"Okay I'll tell her but we'll have to do something to make the house wheelchair accessible."

For some reason Mom seems surprised by that even though I just told her that Robbie is paralyzed.

Some time later we all retire to our rooms. I go up to my childhood bedroom, which hasn't changed a bit since I moved out. I take down one of my old Garfield books from the shelf and smile. I remember when I got this one I stayed up late into the night reading it and laughing so hard that I woke Leah up in the next room.

I read it again and then get out my laptop to do some work. In the morning I'll go to some temple services and then head home.

Jack

I pity these other guys who are not taking their recovery as seriously as me. I am in the physical therapy room nearly every waking hour and doing at least three times as much physical therapy as any of the other patients. Those fools are barely even trying. I am going to succeed from my own will power. I refuse to be defeated.

I've got a pretty good rhythm going now with my days and I fit in both work and physio. When I finish dinner in the evenings Becca often comes to my room and knits while we talk.

Like everyone else she asks when I'm going to order a proper wheelchair and I just say I can't go back to the bank in a wheelchair.

Today she's telling me about a new movie she saw a preview for on YouTube. "I can't remember if it's Jason Bateman or Nathan Fillian who stars in it." Her knitting needles click softly as she talks.

"Those are very different people."

"I can never tell them apart. My sister says I can't tell white people apart. Which is funny because I'm white and people use that saying when they are talking about not being able to tell apart people of other races. The doctors say I have mild facial blindness. Which is such a strange concept. What could possibly cause having perfectly good eyesight but not being able to distinguish features? After the doctor said it I realized that I have relied a lot on cues other than faces to recognize people. Like their hairstyle, their voice, the cadence of how they walk."

"Or don't walk as the case may be," I say with a grin.

"There I've gone again talking too much."

"Your sister seems to have a lot of opinions," I observe. To her it might seem like a non-sequitur but I'm starting to suspect her sister is the source of a lot of her insecurities.

"She helps me see myself from an outside perspective, which can be valuable. I'm told I don't have good self awareness."

Dr. Wilson appears in the doorway. She notices Becca there and a look passes between them. If I had to guess I would bet that Becca has been told before not to get friendly with the patients. Nevertheless, the doctor turns to me and says, "Jack, I know that you are eager to finish your time here and go home but I'm not going to be able to release you if you haven't learned any practical life skills. I'm sending Dr. Julia to talk to you tomorrow about why you don't have your own wheelchair yet."

Oh great. I wonder if I can make myself scarce tomorrow and avoid the whole thing. After Dr. Wilson leaves Becca comments, "I still don't understand why you torture yourself with that thing."

I'll admit this chair is annoying. The people with their own wheelchairs have ones where the bar at the bottom for their feet is one solid piece. A footplate they call it. I'm still using the kind you see on TV or old folks homes where there's two completely separate foot rests with several inches between them. I'm finding that's the most challenging part of using this chair. Well that and it's a little big which puts my arms at an awkward angle as I push the rims. It's remarkable how quickly I'm developing opinions about different kinds of wheelchairs and able to see all these differences.

The conversations continue daily. Dr. Julia comes to see me and I hold firm. I don't let slip that my resolve is beginning to wear down. After all these weeks I have still made exactly zero progress in getting any sensation back in my legs. I'm trying not to panic about it, have to think positive to overcome odds. But there is a nagging little voice in my mind that's starting to question whether I might not be walking out of here.

One day in the hall I pass by Becca on my way to the group therapy. As always I ask her to tell me a joke and she laughs. As I continue on, though, I don't notice that one of my feet has fallen between the two foot rests of the wheelchair until it gets caught underneath and when I push forward my foot catches and I catapult straight out of the seat to face plant on the floor.

I just lay there for a moment feeling stupid but it doesn't take long for staff to rush over to help me. Then I hear Becca's voice. Of course she had to witness my wipeout.

"This is why you need a proper wheelchair," she says.

"Thanks," I say from the floor. "That's real helpful."

"Is it really?"

"No, of course not."

One of the PTs heaves me up off the floor and deposits me back on the wheelchair seat. Becca's face is crestfallen but I'm too busy feeling sorry for myself to reassure her.

"Everything okay?" The PT says, though she's already giving me a pat down to check for injuries. The only thing broken is my pride.

So in the future I come up with a strategy to fix this problem. I take one of my ties and loop it around my ankles and the front rigging of the chair creating a circle that keeps my feet from falling. It might look funny but it works.

When Bill sees it he shakes his head and mutters something about cutting off your nose to spite your face.

Becca

Jack is too stubborn for his own good. It's time to get some advice from Sam about how to help him move forward with his life. With all the time she's spending with Robbie she must have some ideas.

At my next trip to the grocery store to see her I try to broach the topic in a natural way. I fail entirely, of course.

"I have this friend," I begin.

"Oh?" Sam's interest is piqued immediately. "A friend of the male variety by any chance?"

"Yes, but that's not the point right now."

"Okay, I'm listening. Go on."

"He's one of the guys at the rehab center and he's having a particularly difficult time with the transition from able-bodied to disabled. I thought that your boyfriend might have some advice or insight that could help him. At this point he's literally hurting himself."

"Robbie isn't my boyfriend." I notice that she blushes as she says it and tucks a strand of hair behind her ear. Sam herself told me that sometimes people are not truthful because they aren't ready to accept the truth. I think this is one of those times. I don't push it.

"But do you think he could help Jack?"

Sam leans against the cash register and thinks. Then she says, "The thing that Robbie says a lot is that sports transformed his life. He's a big advocate for newly disabled people to get involved in adaptive sports to help them see the possibilities in their lives again."

I consider this. It's hard to imagine Jack playing basketball. I'm not sure he even owns gym clothes. He wears collared polo shirts to physical therapy.

Sam continues, "Actually there's the new sled hockey team that Robbie joined. His sister's boyfriend runs it. They only have four people so they could really use another team member. You should have him check it out."

"That's the same group of guys that organized your rescue, isn't it? I met with them a bunch of times."

"That's right. Robbie calls them the 'wheelchair mafia' now. I'm sure Jack would be welcome to join the club."

"That sounds like a great idea."

"How is the eye contact going?"

"Not great. I'll have to keep practicing." I don't mind that it takes time to perfect these kind of things. I always figure, what would be the point of living if we had it all perfect? If we run out of projects for growth and learning, we may as well just die.

Jack

My friends have finally come to see me. I really wanted to hold that off until I was better but it's taking longer than anticipated. Brooks and Hunter round the corner into my room and Brooks stops short so hard that Hunter runs into his back. I hate that I have to look up at them. I'm taller than both of them. Or I used to be.

"Hey," Brooks says, his voice almost cracking.

Hunter is bolder. He says, "We heard you were in rough shape, man, but sheesh."

I try not to feel insulted. I probably would have said the same thing if our positions were reversed.

“Ha. Yeah,” I say, breaking out my most charming smile.

The mood turns awkward immediately and none of us can think of anything to say. They don't end up staying long. Hunter slaps me on the shoulder and says, "You should join us at the Vineyard when you're back on your feet."

“I’ll do that.”

I'll be honest, I miss weekends on Martha's Vineyard. I miss my real life. So why am I just sitting here? Time to get back to the physio room and keep on working to get it back.

After another hour workout I catch sight of Becca and change course to intercept her. Becca time is just what I need right now. She never fails to entertain me. "What's up?" I say.

"I need to get more cups, want to come with me?"

"Absolutely." I'm glad she doesn't ask me how I am. I want a distraction from thinking about myself. And I know just how to get her talking more. "How is the veil going?"

"It's coming along. I'm starting to feel the time pressure. I'm not sure I'll be able to complete the full border as intended. I'm also realizing that I might not have a big enough space in my apartment to block it."

"What does blocking mean?" I push my wheelchair beside her as she walks and she's completely absorbed in the topic, a tiny wrinkle appearing between her eyebrows.

"So a lot of times when you knit or crochet something the yarn ends up a bit crunched up and blocking allows you to spread it out, get the stitches even, and get the whole project looking far more crisp and nice. It's pretty simple. You get it wet and then stretch it into the shape you want and pin it. When it dries it holds that pinned shape. So with this veil it's a very large lace square and the lace won't show up right without blocking but I need the space to be able to stretch and pin it to its full width."

"I see. Are there tools people use for this?"

"There are blocking boards. I suppose there must be one big enough for a lace shawl project. That's what this pattern really is, a shetland lace shawl but I'm repurposing it as a wedding veil."

Part of my job is asking the right questions and I love that I can get Becca going on a topic.

In the supply room Becca drags a chair over to stand on to reach the top shelf of a cabinet. I'm frustrated that I can't be suave and reach the cups for her. I have to just sit by and watch.

But then Becca starts passing stacks of red solo cups to me and I pile them up on my lap so I guess I'm helping.

"I had an idea for you," Becca says.

"You did?" It's touching that she's been thinking about me. "What kind of idea?"

"Don't be mad."

Oh great. Has anything good ever come after those words?

She continues. "I know that you haven't wanted to do anything that gives in to your disability at all."

I can't help cringing. I don't have a disability, I have a temporary setback that I will overcome. But I don't say anything.

"There's this new hockey team in town that's for people with mobility disabilities and my best friend's boyfriend loves it. He's a wheelchair user and he says sports are great for helping you feel connected to your life again."

"I've never really been a sports guy," I say. Truth be told I have avoided anything that messes up my hair or makes me feel or look less than fresh.

"I think you should give it a chance."

How can I say no to those big brown doe eyes?

"I'll check it out," I promise. And I will. I'm true to my word.

With Christmas right around the corner I'm getting more visitors. Next is my dad whose main purpose is to make sure that I'm still coming to my aunt's house. He doesn't ask, he just says, "You'll be at Jan's for Christmas, of course. We can pick you up."

I guess I have to face people at some point. I can't delay any longer. This is going to be hard. I want to stay positive but I can just barely feel the top of my stomach where it's churning with anxiety.

Thatcher empties out considerably in the week leading up to Christmas. Everyone is visiting home. My dad comes to pick me up Christmas eve. One of the nurses has to help me get into the car with a transfer board. It's just a smooth piece of wood that you use to slide from wheelchair to car and vice versa. She folds the wheelchair and puts it in the trunk of the car then leaves the transfer board with me. I'm supposed to learn how to make these kinds of transfers without it but I'm not wasting time on wheelchair skills when I can be working on healing.

The drive out to Jan's is quiet. Dad has Handal's Messiah playing on the car radio and we don't speak. This is my first time back in a car after my accident if you don't count the short bus that brought me from Mass General to Thatcher. This feels far more similar to the circumstances of my accident. I didn't think riding in Dad's car would affect me that much but I'm feeling very tense. I flinch any time a car comes close to us. I thought I was stronger than this and I hope that my father doesn't notice my reactions. It's been a while since I thought about seeing that truck coming straight for me. It plays in my mind now and by the time we get to my aunt's house my composure has been shredded. It's taking all of my energy to hold myself together.

Dad unfolds the wheelchair from the trunk and brings it to the side of the car. I can see a long line of other cars along the street. There's lots of people here already. I manage to get out of the car and arrange my feet on the foot plates. Yes, with my silk tie holding them on. I will say that my shoes get far less scuffed when I'm not walking on them. My wingtips look pristine and I haven't needed to polish them since my accident.

I'm wearing my best blue suit that brings out the color of my eyes. It's a bit ruined by the way the wheelchair forces me to sit with my knees spread wide apart. One thing I do like about the nicer wheelchairs the other guys have is they make for a tidier look.

There's a light cover of snow on the ground but the sidewalk is thankfully clear. I push off toward Jan's house with every imperfection jostling me. At the house my father has to hoist me over the stoop. I see him wipe sweat from his brow and I feel a pang of guilt. He's too old for this physical effort.

Me showing up causes a huge fuss. The moment I enter the low-ceilinged old living room every face turns toward me.

There's murmurs and tut tut noises. Elderly relatives scramble out of their seats to make room for me. I've never felt so self conscious as I'm moving with every eye on me.

I park next to a sofa where my sister and her fiance are sitting. Lilly smiles and puts her hand on my knee as she says, "It's so good to see you, Jack."

Her partner, Ross, stays leaning back on the sofa with a plate of cornichon. He nods at me and says, “How long do they think you’ll need that thing?”

“They’re not sure,” I lie. The doctors have been perfectly clear about how long they think I’ll need the wheelchair.

“Your dad told us what happened. You should sue the pants off that truck driver.”

I just nod even though I know there’s no money there. It makes people feel better to take some action. To imagine we can restore justice by punishing someone. The truck driver had a heart attack and died while driving. No one left to punish. Just me living a life sentence.

The Christmas tree gives a unique ambiance to the room. As always it is decorated in only white. White lights, white ornaments, and white garland with a crochet angel at the top. The crochet makes me think of Becca and her knitting for a moment and I smile.

I hear a great-aunt asking a cousin who I am in a shaking voice.

"That's Jack. Remember? The oldest of the Baxter boys?"

She nods but doesn't look like she remembers anything.

Jan appears in the doorway to the dining room wearing a ruffled Christmas apron over her red cashmere sweater and chinos. Pearl earrings peek out from her coiffed blonde bob. "Dinner is ready, everyone."

There's a slow press of bodies from the living room to the dining table. I hold back until everyone else has moved out of the way. When I approach the table Jan puts her hand on my shoulder and says, "Jack, I've put you over on this side next to your mother."

"Merry Christmas, darling," Mom says as I pull in next to her. It's a tight squeeze but I fit.

"Merry Christmas," I return with a kiss on her cheek.

Directly across from us my two brothers begin the one-upmanship. I'm the oldest, then it's Don, followed by Josh, and finally our sister Lilly.

“Just one slice of ham for me,” Don says. “Need to fit into my suit when I give the keynote speech at the national sales conference.”

"Oh that reminds me," Josh says, "I'm starting my new role after Christmas. I was just promoted and I'm now the youngest VP in my company's history."

I used to participate in the competition too but this year I stay silent. I've had a few accomplishments at work but nothing I feel like bragging about. It's hard not to feel like I'm hopelessly in negative points until I can brag about overcoming a spinal cord injury that doctors predicted was impossible.

People keep sneaking looks at me. I hate being the center of attention. This is exhausting and I find myself wishing I were back at the rehab center.

After dinner the serious drinks come out. Most of my relatives hold their liquor well and you'd never know they were drinking at all. But my brothers get entirely sloshed along with my soon-to-be brother-in-law.

Everyone sits around the living room pulling chocolates and oranges from stockings embroidered with snowflakes and reindeer. For a moment everything is cozy and warm and comforting.

As darkness falls, the younger generation gathers out in the backyard. The porch lights illuminate our faces while the rest of the yard is full of looming shadows of trees. Every so often a bit of wind knocks some snow from a tree branch and it glows in the lamplight until it hits the ground.

"Guess I'm finally going to win the New Year's egg race now that you're incapacitated," Don says, nearly falling over with laughter.

"Don't count on it," I return.

"Think you'll be running by then?" Josh asks in complete sincerity. New Year's is like a week from now, what is he thinking?

"No, I'll put the egg on my lap."

Lilly has gone back inside but Ross is out here with us. "Here's something I always wondered," he says, a glass bottle of beer dangling from his fingers, "when they say 'paralyzed from the waist down', does that mean *everything* below the belt?"

Josh looks properly shocked and smacks Ross's upper arm. "Hey, man, that's not cool."

"How many paraplegics do you know that you've always wondered that?" I say.

"What? I'm not allowed to ask questions? Educate me, I just want to learn."

"Is this your way of saying you want to sleep with me?" I say with a smirk and Don laughs so hard he spits his beer into the snow.

"Fine, be an asshole," Ross mutters but he drops the subject. There is no way in hell I'm going to tell Ross that I can't feel my dick and need a catheter to pee still. That's the worst indignity of this entire situation.

My father pokes his head out the door. "It's about time we should be getting you back," he says.

"Wouldn't want you to miss your bedtime," Ross says. "Make sure they tuck you in well."

Dad frowns and looks utterly perplexed by the comment. I don't say anything but follow Dad back through the house and out to the car. In the end I am glad that I came. It's been a nice break spending time with my siblings and messing with Ross.

Becca

Jack and I are sitting outside on the Thatcher lawn even though it's cold. The weather is unpredictable and almost all hints of snow are gone today. You can just see a mound of dirty ice and snow at the edge of the parking lot where the plow pushed it.

I tried to put a blanket on Jack's lap but he said, "Absolutely not" and we aren't staying out very long anyway. I'm waiting on my date to pick me up.

I'm sitting on a bench with Jack next to me in the center's wheelchair. I've got my knitting out. I'm running out of time to get this veil finished.

"How does it get its shape?" Jack says.

"What?"

"Your knitting."

"Oh! Well, you see knitting is a process of pulling loops through other loops and the width of the project is determined by how many loops you put on the needles, while the length is determined by how long you knit for. Clearly you can manipulate the factor of how long you knit for but you can also manipulate the width because you can close off loops by pulling one loop through two previous loops instead of one and you can add loops. The needles are the tools to make the loops go through each other and there's lots of different diameters of knitting needles, which makes the loops bigger or smaller. A project with small loops will be tightly knit, while a project with big loops will be looser but also you'll get more length quickly. Then the lace is accomplished by patterns of holes and increasing and decreasing the loops."

I pause for a breath and try to figure out if he's bored by my explanation of knitting. He doesn't look bored to me but I don't have the best track record of guessing on that.

"So you have very small needles and small stitches but the project is still lace," Jack says.

"Yes. That's the holes that are strategically placed to create a pattern but the individual stitches are all small." I hold it out where he can see the tiny loops. "I prefer what they call small gauge projects but the big bulky projects have been in fashion. I'm not boring you, am I?"

"Not at all." He smiles and I feel a strange sensation of heat in my belly. "I love hearing about people's hobbies," Jack continues. "You learn so much from listening."

It makes me happy to hear that. I try to censor myself because I've been told enough times that "no one wants to hear everything you know about fill-in-the-blank." But it takes effort to clamp down the urge to share my interests. I feel so relaxed around Jack.

Then I see Paul striding up the path towards us and I sigh.

"That's my date," I say, standing up.

"Ready?" Paul says when he reaches us. He doesn't even glance at Jack but I make introductions.

"Paul, this is my friend Jack. Jack, this is Paul. My mom thinks we would be perfect together because we're both autistic."

Jack laughs but I can't figure out what was funny. As much as I study comedy and jokes there are still times when I can't figure out what makes something funny. There's clearly more to learn.

"Hi, man," Jack says, holding out his hand to shake.

Paul frowns but shakes his hand. Then he says to me, "Let's go. I have a reservation."

I walk away from Jack reluctantly. I wish I could spend all day hanging out with him.

The restaurant is the same one Paul and I always go to. It does help to go somewhere very familiar to avoid surprises. He always orders the same thing. To be fair, so do I. The staff don't always even bother to ask anymore.

Today Paul is in a fury over something he read in the news. An autistic man lost his job and it's not entirely clear if it's because of his autism or if he was being extremely rude. If you ask Paul there's no difference. He believes that rudeness is an entirely neurotypical idea. I'm not sure where he gets the idea that autistics don't offend each other. From what I've seen we offend each other constantly.

"The neurotypicals need to learn about autism and accommodate us."

"Sure, that would be great. But doesn't it feel futile to try to change the whole world?"

"So you aren't even going to try?"

"I'm trying in smaller ways."

"You're masking. You're giving in to their view of the world. Stop doing that and force them to engage with our world."

"I just believe in meeting people half way."

"You are going more than halfway. You have a self-improvement journal."

He hates how I cater to NTs but why sit in a corner miserable and not even try to meet people halfway?

Paul has a point. I understand where he's coming from. A lot of autistic people are tired of living in a world built for neurotypicals and the expectation that we change ourselves to fit in their systems and social norms. What makes our own social norms and instincts any less correct?

"They need to accommodate us but how will they be forced to do that when people like you just give in?"

We've had this conversation more than once.

"I just think you're living in an ideal world that is never going to actually exist," I say. "And I'd rather practice fitting in and be happy than dig my heels in and be miserable."

Paul is furiously swirling food around on his plate. I continue to try to explain myself. There are few things I hate more than feeling misunderstood. "Yes, I mask and I learn to do the things that neurotypicals want and expect. I do want change but I think demanding full and total change immediately is just going to turn people off. I want to work within the system."

"You're like a pet to them. They train you to obey."

I nod. "That may be." What I don't say is that even if that's true, I seem to be living a more peaceful and happy life than Paul is. He and I are the perfect example of why autistic people don't just automatically get along with other autistic people. My mom continues to try to push us together and just as Paul says, I acquiesce to her and continue to go on these ridiculous dates.

Paul huffs and then we just eat in silence.

It's not that I don't want a partner and to find love. I'm just not sure how to go about it and none of the men I've ever been interested in have been able to stand me for very long. Could Jack be different? He doesn't seem different, he seems like the most aggressively neurotypical person I've ever met. The time we spend together is in a bubble outside of the real world and he is trying to get back to that world.

As much as we spend a lot of time together, I think I'm just an amusing distraction for him while he fights to get better. I do wish he understood that he can improve his life from where he's at now. I've been volunteering at Thatcher for a very long time and I've seen a lot of spinal cord injuries. Some things can't be fixed by just trying harder.

A tough lesson for anyone to accept.

Before long Jack will have to end his time in rehab and go back to his real life. I doubt he'll find time for me then. I'm going to miss him a lot. A tear threatens to fall from my eye and I force myself to think about something else. Luckily Paul doesn't notice my distress and I occupy myself with thinking through the math for how many repeats of lace pattern I should put on the edge of Leah's veil. By now the veil is so large that it takes me about two hours to make it through a complete round and with the wedding coming up soon I need to think realistically about how many more rounds I have time for.

When I get back to my apartment there is a huge flat rectangular box outside the door. I'm so confused, for a moment I wonder if I've gotten off the elevator on the wrong floor. But no, the package is addressed to me.

I open my door and pull the massive box inside. On the floor I tear open the cardboard and find a folded lace blocking board. For several seconds I just blink at it in shock. Then I dig into the box to find a paper with a note. It's from Jack.

What an incredibly thoughtful gift. He really does listen when I ramble on about knitting. It's so nice to be able to just talk about it as much as I want. I don't have any idea how I can thank him. But I better get working on the veil so I can put the board to good use and take a picture to show him.

Jack

Becca leads me deeper into the gym and I will admit that I don't mind watching her ass in her corduroy pants while she walks.

No sooner do I push into the ice rink room than I see Carly.

A few months ago in an entirely different lifetime, in an entirely different world, I went on a date with her and attended a fundraiser for her charity. Fuck. Now that I think about it, the charity was raising money to create this very hockey program.

The pain of flipping to the other side of the cause is indescribable.

Carly sees me. She stares. "Jack?!" she says incredulously.

What can I even say? "Yep," I say.

"I almost didn't even recognize you! A lot has clearly changed since the last time we saw each other."

"Yeah, I got hit by a truck."

"Oh my God!"

"You know each other?" Becca chimes in with surprise.

"We've met," I say and leave it at that.

Oh and there's the other guy Carly was mooning over at the fundraising dinner. He was walking with a cane at the event but now he's in a wheelchair and I can see that both his legs are almost entirely gone. You can tell instantly looking at him that he's ex-military.

"Welcome," he says, holding out a strong veiny hand to shake. "I'm Murph."

"Jack," I say. Though we've been introduced before I don't think either of us remembered the other's name.

Becca pulls over another woman with long silky brown hair and says, "This is my best friend, Sam."

"Hi, Jack, great to meet you. Becca has lovely things to say about you."

Murph points to the ice and names the three dudes pushing sleds around with short hockey sticks. "We've got Rob, Danny, and Mark out there."

I'm already feeling on edge from seeing Carly and Murph in this completely different context. Even though Carly and I didn't hit it off, I still have a competitive urge with her boyfriend. I don't like losing, regardless of the circumstances. I know that's stupid but there's no way I'm going to let myself be vulnerable in front of this guy and try something new that I'm sure to suck at.

I back away. "I don't think this is for me," I say.

"Listen, man, every one of the guys knows what you're going through."

I can't help thinking: what does a jarhead know about what I'm dealing with? I can see all the doors of the life I built for myself shutting in my face.

In a world where appearance is reality, there is no place for a broken body.

It doesn't take long for me to realize that Becca has no idea that I'm pissed at her. I'm being frosty but she's chatting away as normal. And I'm almost sucked into it, wanting to ask questions about the knitting. But no, this is serious.

"Becca."

"Yeah?"

"I'm not doing that hockey thing."

"Okay."

"No, like, I do not want you pushing me to do cripple things."

She puts down the knitting on her lap and looks at me, a wrinkle in the center of her forehead. "That's not exactly what I'd call it," she says. She picks her yarn back up and says down to it, "You're being very sisyphean right now."

"I'm what?"

"Pushing a rock that's going to roll back down the mountain, making no progress."

No progress? This is the level of hard work it takes to get better and I'm not going to let anyone stop me. All my hours in the gym are going to pay off. "I can't give up on walking," I say.

"Why not?"

That question throws me. To anyone else it would be obvious. Sometimes the things Becca says bewilder me and honestly I keep coming back to see how she'll bewilder me next. How do I put into words what should be obvious to anyone?

"I'm not the kind of person who shrugs and gives up. I'm not okay with laziness or failing. I can't just sit in a wheelchair all day and wait to die." My throat feels tight. I don't want to even face the possibility of that.

"What are you talking about giving up? That's ridiculous. Every day you are overcoming challenges most people never have to deal with. Every day that you get up and live your life in a wheelchair is a day that you have succeeded. Getting your feeling back is not the measure of success. Walking is not the measure of success. You saw Robbie and Murph. They are not sitting in a wheelchair all day waiting to die. Doing what you want to do in life no matter how challenging your body makes it for you is success. I mean, how many people have ever worked half as hard as you have in the last few months? That's not lazy. Accepting yourself how you are is okay too."

"I could say the same to you," I spit out. I know all about her self-improvement journal and how hard she works at changing herself.

The knitting is once again forgotten and falls to the floor as she gets up. Her voice gets louder and I feel a strange urge to hurt her feelings. I don't know why. I want to make her feel the pain that I'm feeling now.

She says, "I used to get meltdowns every time I went to the grocery store but I kept practicing until it became a familiar and comfortable place. That's the difference. I'm not trying to be something other than what I am, I'm trying to learn strategies to manage the world as I am. I know that I'm autistic and I'm never not going to be. You need to learn that you're a paraplegic and you're never not going to be but you can get better and better at being in the world as a paraplegic."

"No that's not who I am. I'm Jack, I'm a banker, I'm going to stand as a groomsman at my sister's wedding next year. Stop trying to make me a better person. I do not in fact have to accept any of this shit. What I need is to find the right doctor to fix this."

"What if you can't?"

"Get out," I shout.

She sweeps the yarn up off the floor and into her bag and runs from the room. I feel so angry and all the emotion is trapped in my body. I have to prove Becca wrong and the doctors wrong. I need to redouble my efforts.

I push off to the physio room. At this hour it's empty and dark but the door isn't locked. I go straight to the parallel bars. I've done this enough now that I know how to strap the long metal leg braces on myself. I get them on and my legs stretch out straight in front of me, held rigid by the braces. My wheelchair is positioned at one end of the parallel bars and I reach up to grip one in each hand. It takes every ounce of my strength to heave myself up to a standing position and the bars shake slightly as I hold all of my weight up with them.

I try to visualize the nerves in my spine regrowing and reconnecting. If manifestation works, now is the time. "Come on, legs, you remember what to do," I whisper. They don't move.

Instead I use what's left of my core muscles to pull the legs forward. I make my way down the length of the parallel bars using my arms to swing my lower body forward. I've done this multiple times a day every day and while my arms have gotten much stronger since I've been at Thatcher, there's no change in my legs. What more do I need to do? What will it take?

In the empty silent room my grunts and the bang of my feet each time I move forward echoes off the walls. Fueled by my anger and frustration I move faster. There's a rhythm to this exercise. Shift hands farther out on the cold metal, hold tight and use all the strength in my shoulders and arms to swing my metal-encased legs forward to land on the floor beneath me.

I reach the end of the bars and now I need to turn and go all the way back where the empty wheelchair is waiting. The turn is the trickiest part and I have to admit my muscles are starting to get worn out and I feel my upper arms trembling.

"Keep going, you lazy bastard," I hiss to myself.

With a deep breath I swiftly move my left hand to the same bar as my right hand and pause there before moving my right hand to the left bar and straightening out my body. I did it. A surge of pride swells in my chest.

Then my right wrist buckles and I crash straight to the floor with my arm pinned under my back. Ouch.

I'm completely stuck. The wheelchair may as well be a million miles away. I can't do anything but wait for someone to rescue me. If there were a fire in the building right now I'd be able to do absolutely nothing to save myself. I've never felt so betrayed by my body.

With the blood flow to my arm restricted it falls asleep too and now more than half my body is numb. Eventually I drift off on the floor from sheer exhaustion.

"Jack Baxter, what have you done?" A stern voice awakens me and I blearily open my eyes to see Bill standing over me with his arms folded over his chest.

"Early morning workout?"

He sighs and kneels down to gently guide my arm out from under me. "You know this isn't helping you, Jack. It's just going to set you back. We'll have to get your arm checked out and you might even end up on bed rest. I know you want to work hard, but you can hurt yourself if you work too hard."

I've heard it all before. Bill sees that he's not getting through to me so he goes to get the wheelchair. He unstraps the braces around my legs and then picks me up like a rag doll and places me back on the chair. Now the pins and needles are starting in my arm and it hurts like hell. I bite my lip and since I can't use my arm to wheel myself, Bill pushes me back to my room and gets me into bed.

Becca

I am sad that Jack still doesn't want to adjust to the life situation he has landed in. It's frustrating to see him struggling more than he needs to. I wish I could just download into his brain the way I see it.

Sometimes I feel like an alien trying to learn the customs of earthlings. I feel so distant and disconnected from other people. But there's no home planet for me to return to. I have to keep trying to manage life here on this planet no matter how exhausting it is.

The veil is finished. I blocked it overnight and texted the picture to Jack but he didn't respond. I think I've ruined things with him. I was only trying to help but of course because it's me it did the opposite of helping.

It's hard in moments like this not to feel like the world would be better off without me. I've said it before and Sam always insists that she needs me. I can't see what it is she sees in me. All I do is screw things up and make people upset.

Since I'm alone in my apartment I give in to some tears. I whisper to myself, "I hate you. Why can't you be normal?" It doesn't take long before I'm banging my forehead against the wall in a regular beat. It's hard to explain how the pain feels good. I continue to repeat "I hate you" to myself over and over until I wear myself out and slump on the cold floor.

Then I remind myself that dying the week before her wedding is only going to make Leah more upset and pull myself together.

I need to drive the veil down to Connecticut. I'm feeling something about that but I don't know what it is so I push past it. I rub the tears from my face and start driving.

At my parents' house nothing is as normal. With the wedding less than a week away everyone is in a frenzy. Larry has already gone back to Alabama where the wedding is taking place. Leah is here running back and forth, searching for things, throwing things in bags.

I feel like maybe I shouldn't be here. I'm just going to get in the way.

"Is this it?" Mom grabs hold of the veil and shows it off to Dad and Leah. "Would you look at this? It's beautiful, Becca." She continues to marvel over it and I can't tell how Leah herself feels about it. Her facial expressions have always been completely unreadable to me.

All I can do is hope she likes it. And my feelings of worthlessness are bubbling back up so I quietly excuse myself and go up to my room alone.

I end up sitting in the center of my bed with my arms wrapped around my knees just staring blankly at the wall. I think something is processing in me so I just let it happen. One phrase keeps circling in my mind over and over. *You're a failure of a human being.*

Jack

I haven't talked to Becca since I yelled at her. I haven't even seen her around Thatcher like I usually do. I am starting to feel bad about our fight. Then to my surprise her number comes up on my phone.

Even though I'm eyeballs deep in a work project on my laptop I answer right away.

The instant I hit the button I hear Becca's frantic voice. "Jack? I need you. I'm about to have a meltdown."

"Where are you?"

"Logan." And the phone goes dead.

Fuck. How am I going to get to the airport?

Panic immediately grips me. I heard the plea in her voice and I can think about nothing except how to get to her and make sure she's okay. I search for a cab company on my phone and call them.

"I need a taxi right away. Let the driver know I have a wheelchair but I can get in without help." That's a lie. I have no idea how I'm going to manage that transfer but I don't want them to turn me away. I give them the address and hang up.

I'm going to need to learn what's legal and illegal when it comes to how people in wheelchairs are treated so I know what I can push for. For now I just need to get to Becca before something bad happens.

Thankfully I am now able to get myself from my bed into the wheelchair. Some things you can't help but learn. I grab my wallet and then one disposable catheter package just in case. I stuff both into a small bag with my phone and rush from the room to the front of Thatcher.

The cab company is true to their word and a taxi has arrived quickly. The driver is a middle aged middle eastern man. He gets out and looks at me skeptically. I hand him my small case then wheel up to the back door and open it. I stare at the seat of the car for a moment.

I am going to fall on my ass. Good thing I can't feel it, I guess.

Why haven't I practiced this more? It's been all about walking and not what I really need. Hours and hours of physical therapy and I'm terrified of trying to get myself from a wheelchair to the car. I'm an idiot.

"Let me give you a hand," the driver says. I want to insist that I can do it but I know that I actually can't so I let him help me. I'm grateful he's willing to but I know going forward I can't count on that.

After he puts the wheelchair in the trunk and gets back behind the wheel he says, "Where to, sir?"

"Logan, please."

He starts driving before asking, "Which airline are you flying? I can bring you to the right door."

"Oh. Actually, I don't know."

"Can you check your reservation?"

I don't want to admit the crazy truth of why I'm going to the airport so I just pick at random and tell him Southwest.

Becca must be flying for her sister's wedding. It's about the right time for that.

If I could I'd be tapping my foot but instead I tap my fingers on my knee. When we hit the traffic in the tunnel I'm ready to burst from the anxiety. Finally I see the signs to Logan and the cab pulls up to one of the departure doors. Once again the driver unfolds my wheelchair and helps me get out of the car.

I pay him and include a large tip.

"Enjoy your trip, sir."

"Thanks," I say. I grab my little bag and push towards the automatic door.

People are looking at me and seeing a disabled man. They don't know this is my first time out in public with a wheelchair. I still see myself as an able bodied man having a bad few months but I can tell that everyone around me sees a man firmly labeled "disabled." But I don't have time to worry about that.

I barrel through the terminal like some kind of goddamn nascar driver. People leap out of my way. I'm focused on one thing only, finding Becca.

It's a big airport but it doesn't take long before I see a commotion in front of me.

It's her. She's on the floor curled up and wailing. Instead of helping, the people nearby are walking a wide berth around her and staring in horror as they go by.

"Becca," I shout. "It's me, Becca. I'm here." She doesn't seem to be connected to reality anymore. Her eyes are unfocused. I skid to a stop at her side and lean over the best I can without toppling out of the wheelchair. "Becca, can you hear me? What can I do?"

The sound she's making is terrifying. My heart is pounding so hard in my chest. As I touch her, she grabs hold of my arm and as scared as I am of being pulled over onto her I try to be strong and reassuring. She clings to me and I wrap my arms around her awkwardly. The wailing has stopped but now she's sobbing into my lap and shaking.

Eventually I hear her whisper, "I'm sorry."

I've never seen anything like what I just witnessed. A grown woman as out of control as a child. But I know her. I know how competent she is. Which just makes this more terrifying. And what I feel most is fury that no one here tried to do anything to help her. I hold her closer. "Don't be sorry, it's not your fault."

She looks up at me with a tear-streaked face and I feel stricken. I just want to fix everything for her.

I nod towards a bench and say, "Let's sit." Is it a weird thing to say when I'm already sitting? I don't know.

She clings to me as we make our way over. Fewer people are staring now. I try to just ignore it and focus on Becca.

"Thank you for coming for me," she says.

"What happened?" I ask.

"I got overwhelmed. I tried to plan out every step of this trip so I wouldn't get scared and lose control but when the machine got jammed and wouldn't print my boarding pass I felt the panic rising and I knew I wasn't going to make it much longer before a meltdown. I tried to call Sam but her phone is off. I didn't know what else to do. When I'm in that state I can't really think rationally."

"Does that happen often?"

She looks to the floor and rubs the toe of one shoe against the tile. "Not anymore. It's really embarrassing and I'm sorry you had to see it."

"It's okay. You scared me but it's not your fault."

She picks at her hand with a fingernail. "Sometimes I wish I was someone else. Anyone else besides myself."

I take the hand she's picking with and hold it. "I don't wish that. How can I enjoy a joke anymore without you there to explain why it's funny?"

She's silent. Eventually I say, "What are you thinking about?"

Very quietly she says towards the floor, "That someday you'll leave Thatcher and go back to your life. Then you'll be fine without my analysis of jokes."

I don't know what to say to that. She's right that I can't quite picture how Becca would fit into my life. I change the subject back to what just happened. "You said it was a meltdown? What does that mean?"

"That's what they call it even though that word makes it sound like I'm a toddler who didn't get her way and that's not it at all. I think it's more like a panic attack but when I've heard people describe panic attacks they say they think they're having a heart attack or that they're dying. Meltdowns don't feel like that. Basically it happens when my ability to cope with sensory input is filled past capacity or the stress of trying to do something new and not in my routine can also overflow it. It's like there's a cup inside me and when it overflows it causes this watershed that shuts down rationality and self-control. Part of my mind can see myself and is embarrassed but I can't do anything to stop the meltdown until it has run its course. It doesn't happen often but sometimes I push myself too hard and overwhelm my ability to cope. And then people treat me like a child."

The look she gives me then makes me want to kiss her fiercely on the lips. But this hardly seems like the right time. She's still trembling a bit. And she's also right that I don't know if we will still be in each other's lives after my time at Thatcher is done.

Becca looks at the time on her phone screen and sighs. “I need to get through security now but I'm scared.” She looks back to me and says, “Please come with me?”

“On the plane? You can't be serious.” Except of course she is. She only analyzes jokes, she doesn't make them. “That's crazy. I don't know the first thing about flying while paralyzed.”

She nods. “I understand,” she says but her voice is shaking and I can tell she's trying as hard as she can to be okay with me saying no. Damn my heart. There's something about this girl that just makes me want to protect her against all unhappiness.

"Could you maybe just escort me as far as security?" her soft voice says.

"All right, did you get the boarding pass to print?"

She nods and holds it out to me. I take note of the security gate and flight number. She stands and puts her hand on my shoulder and goes with me as I head towards the counter.

I'm not going to security yet. I can feel her fingers digging into my shoulder. I think she's still too freaked out to realize that I'm heading the wrong direction.

At the counter the woman has to lean to the side to talk to me. I never noticed before how many little things are unnecessarily difficult in a wheelchair.

"Okay, here's the situation," I say to her. "I need to get on to flight 4423 so I need to get a ticket right now. But I had this injury and I've never flown using a wheelchair before. Can you hook me up?"

She looks back and forth between me and Becca. Probably from her vantage point she saw Becca's breakdown. It's like she can't figure out which one of us is more competent to talk to.

Finally she snaps out of it and starts typing on the keyboard in front of her. "Let me check if there is space on that flight, sir."

I'll never understand why it takes so much time for airport agents to work their computers. How are their machines still so slow in this day and age?

Becca squeezes my shoulder and whispers, "Thank you."

At least there's something I can do to support her as much as she has supported me. Or in theory I can. I still don't have the first idea how to get on an airplane while paralyzed. Maybe I can look up a YouTube video about it at the gate. What a world.

"Yes, I can get you a seat on that plane but there's only one left so I can't put you together from here. You will get priority boarding so speak to the agent at the gate and they can probably arrange things."

I pass my credit card up to her and say, "I appreciate your help."

With a boarding pass in hand I turn to Becca. "Time for security. Also, where are we going?"

"Alabama," she says.

"Why is your sister getting married in Alabama?"

"That's where her fiance is from."

"There are Jews in Alabama?"

"Sure are."

"Learn something new every day," I mutter.

We weave through the security line, Becca staying as close to me as she can. When we reach the front of the line one of the attendants checks our IDs and then says to me, "Can you stand at all?"

"No." It's a punch in the gut every time I have to say it.

They separate me from Becca and I'm anxiously watching, afraid to leave her alone for a second, especially in this environment. I don't know how to explain it to them but in this moment I think she's more disabled than I am.

She's frozen to the spot for a moment but then her memory of what to do kicks in and she starts taking off her shoes to put on the conveyor belt while I'm being physically patted down. They check the wheelchair the way they do laptops with the wand.

I guess it's fair that the staff all assume I know how my own disability works. But when it comes to flying paralyzed, they are the experts. Or we're all equally ignorant and I'll be lucky to arrive in Alabama in one piece. Why am I so ill prepared? Oh yeah, I've spent the last couple months focused only on walking and I've got nothing to show for it. Can't even move a toe.

At the gate I talk to the agent about seating and having Becca with me. In my mind I'm here to help her but I'm sure they think she's here to help me. They move things around, talk to some people, and tell me not to worry.

I can't imagine how this is ever going to work. There is no way this wheelchair is making it to a seat on the plane. Even if I had ordered a custom wheelchair I'm certain that wouldn't fit either.

Becca and I sit side by side in the gate area silently. Each of us is wrapped up in our own worries. When the announcement goes out for pre-boarding one of the agents approaches me. "We have an aisle chair waiting for you, if you'll follow me."

I don't know what that is but Becca and I follow him, skirting around a family of five with young kids trying to run in all different directions. Just outside the plane door there is a skinny red chair with wheels on the bottom and a seatbelt hanging loosely off a black seat.

"If you'll just transfer over to this chair we will stow your wheelchair with the luggage and have it waiting for you when you disembark."

Oh joy. More transfers. The surface area of the aisle chair is so narrow that I'm certain I'll fall if I try to get my paralyzed butt onto it.

"Um, Becca, can you help?"

"Of course. What can I do?"

I look at the puzzle in front of me and strategize. "Okay, I'm going to put my feet down first and then put one arm around your shoulder."

The gate agent is looking at us like he's wishing he made me sign a waiver.

I hold onto the back of the wheelchair with one hand while I lean forward and undo the tie around my legs. Then I lift each foot onto the ground in front of the aisle chair. A slight tremor goes through both legs but they mostly stay in place.

With my hands I push my body to the front edge of my chair and reach out for Becca. She's so tiny she doesn't even have to lean over for me to get my arm around her shoulders. She wraps one of her arms around my waist and I plant my other hand on the aisle chair seat.

"On three," I say. Then I count. "One. Two. Three." Together we swing my body over. And it works. I slump back against the tall back of the aisle chair in relief. The gate agent straps the seatbelt on me and Becca checks that my feet are in place. The agent pushes me onto the plane. There's a little jolt as we go over the doorway but I'm securely in place. Becca follows behind and he stops at the first row of seats.

That front row gives us a little more room to maneuver so Becca can help me get back out of the aisle chair and into a seat. For all that work I spent about a minute and a half in the thing.

Over the next few minutes the plane begins to fill up with people. A man in a suit and tie sits next to us, taking the window seat. He immediately pulls out a laptop and he's still on the phone with someone on Bluetooth headphones. I look at him and see a ghost of myself. That has been me so many times before.

He of course doesn't even glance at me. Even though I'm not in the wheelchair right now I know that he would never see himself in me. How arrogant we are, believing that we're on top of the world because of our talents and drive. It can all disappear in a second, revealing that we were never in control of our success. Not fully anyway.

The plane rumbles and begins rolling towards the tarmac. Beside me Becca's foot is tapping relentlessly on the floor of the plane, which reverberates through the seats.

"You okay there?" I ask.

"I don't like flying."

I could have told you that. Clearly she struggles whenever she's out of her comfort zone so unless her job has her flying every two days she's bound to be stressed about it.

"Tell me about your family that we're going to see," I say to take her mind off it.

"I don’t know what to tell you.”

The question is too open-ended. I need to narrow it down for her.

"So I know your sister is older than you. Then there's what, your mom and dad?"

"Yes that's right."

"Do you like the man your sister is marrying?"

Becca shrugs. "He's fine. Seems like a good match for her, anyway."

As the plane reaches cruising altitude I realize no one around me knows I can't feel or move anything below my waist. This is great. I'm just like my old self. I flag down a flight attendant.

"Bring a jack daniels, would you darling?"

When the flight attendant walks away I wink at Becca and say, "A Jack for Jack."

She doesn't smile.

What can I do to cheer her up? I get my drink and while I'm sipping on it she whispers, "I'm sorry I made you go to hockey. I shouldn't have pushed. It was none of my business."

I put the drink down on my tray. "I over reacted," I say, looking her square in the face even though she isn't meeting my eyes. "I know you want to help. I'm sure you understand that it's very hard to deal with everything that's happened to me."

"I obviously can't say I know what it's like but I have seen a lot of people over the years go through the process."

I swirl my drink thoughtfully. "And they all make it through to the other side in the end?"

She nods. "They do. And you know I never lie."

"Then I'll trust you that I'm going to find equilibrium again."

Only moments later the plane begins its descent. The flight from Boston to Huntsville is not all that long. Another flight attendant comes over to us and says, "If you'll wait until all the other passengers have disembarked we can get an aisle chair to you."

I nod. And so we wait after the plane lands until all the other passengers have gotten off and then we go through the whole aisle chair thing in reverse. My ugly-ass wheelchair is waiting just outside the plane and then Becca and I come out into the Huntsville airport terminal.

Becca says, "I always meet my mother at baggage claim even though I don't have a checked bag."

"You don't have a checked bag?" Yet another thing she's said that bewilders me. When I travel I usually bring an entire matching set of three pieces of luggage.

"Just my backpack," she says, hoisting the strap on her shoulder.

"Huh. On a different note, will you be okay if I stop at the bathroom?"

"Oh that's a good idea. Yes, I'll just text my mom that I've landed."

Since we were the last ones off the plane the rush for the bathrooms has already passed and there's no lines. We veer off into the respective sides and take care of that business. But I didn't pack for a trip and I only have the one cath. I'm going to have to make this one last until I can buy more. Though it's meant to be disposable I carefully wash it out with soap and water and put it back into its plastic packaging.

On the way to baggage claim we have to find an elevator while everyone else is going down the escalator or stairs. I've heard rumors of people going down escalators in wheelchairs but we all know I am not skilled enough to attempt anything that reckless.

As we search for the elevator I see Becca's tension rising. She's starting to get agitated again. "Hey," I say, reaching for her fingers. "I'm here with you. We're in this together and we're going to be fine." I don't mention that if I weren't here she wouldn't be having to hunt down an elevator.

We find the elevator and go down with a mom who has a stroller and an airline attendant pushing an elderly woman in an airport wheelchair, which is markedly different from mine or any other one I've ever seen.

As the doors open I see a middle aged woman who looks exactly like Becca. She catches sight of us and rushes over to squeeze Becca in her arms. "I watched every person from your flight come through and leave. What took you so long? You almost gave me a stroke."

"Mom, this is my friend Jack."

Becca's mom notices me for the first time and she frowns. "What do you mean?" she says. She's probably imagining that Becca just made friends with me in the last ten minutes walking through the terminal.

"He came with me," she says. "I was having some trouble at the airport and Jack came along to help me."

Mrs. Cohen doesn't spend too long trying to figure that one out. Clearly she's used to her daughter's unique approach to life. "You must be one of her patients at the rehab?"

Kind of a weird way to put it since Becca is a volunteer there and not a nurse or a doctor but I guess that's close enough. "Yeah, basically," I say.

"Well, let's get you checked in at the hotel, Bec. Sorry, what did you say was?"

"I'm Jack. Jack Baxter."

"Are you staying at the same hotel?"

"Uh. Hopefully."

Her mom sighs and then we all head outside to get a ride. This time at least I know that Becca can help me get in and out of the car. Who's helping who here? No one knows.

By now I am so exhausted I don't even have the words for it. This has been an incredibly long day of physical challenges. I need to stretch out my aching back on a soft bed and sleep for a week and a half.

I know there's at least one more challenge facing me when we get to the hotel. Will they have any rooms available? Will they have an accessible room available?

Becca must be worn out too. That episode she had took a lot out of her, I can tell. And she's strung tight with nerves now, probably worried about her family and the wedding. If I had more energy I would try to get her talking about one of her favorite subjects but my brain is fried.

At the hotel Mrs. Cohen gets herself and Becca checked into their rooms but then Becca tells her to go ahead because she wants to help me get situated. Once she's out of earshot I turn on every bit of charm I can muster and ask the hotel receptionist about free rooms.

"There's a wedding this weekend, sir, and all the rooms have been booked for weeks."

"I suppose that includes the accessible rooms as well?"

"Yes, I'm afraid so. I believe some elderly relatives are in that room."

Right, of course there's only one wheelchair accessible room. Just like bathroom stalls, if it's occupied then I'm just shit out of luck.

“I don’t mind sharing my hotel room if you don’t mind,” Becca says.

"Are we going to scandalize your family?"

Becca shrugs. "They don't have to know."

With her mom staying on the same floor I’m not entirely convinced that’s possible but I’m too tired to say no to the offer.

She gets the keycards and we follow the signs to the room.

Becca holds the door open. I try to follow her into the room and almost crush my hands in the doorframe. I stop short.

"I don't think I'm going to fit," I say.

Becca bends down and examines how close my wheel rims are to the door edges. "I think you'll fit if you keep your hands in your lap and I push you through."

"Okay, let's try." If this doesn't work I don't know what I'll do. Sleep in the hallway probably. And have the police called on me.

Becca and I exchange places and she gets behind me. I hold the door open in front of me and she shoves the wheelchair through.

"Yes!" Becca says, very pleased with the result.

I'm relieved to see there are two twin beds in the room. I head straight for the first one and grab fistfulls of the duvet to hoist myself up. "Oh my God that feels good," I say as I collapse back on the mattress.

Becca grabs my ankles and pulls them further up on the bed. Probably a good idea. I did the bare minimum and could have slipped back off.

It's now that I realize I didn't think I was taking a trip so I didn't pack any of my medications. Hopefully I'll be okay one night without my blood thinner and anti-spasm medicine because I fall asleep almost instantly.

When I wake again I'm alone and the room is dark. There's a text on my phone from Becca saying she's gone to the rehearsal dinner and will be back soon. That's all the permission I need to fall fast asleep again.

The whole night goes like that. I wake for a moment, assess my surroundings, and fall back asleep.

In the morning I'm woken by light coming through the blinds and look over to see Becca still asleep on the other bed. She's tucked herself into a ball and her mess of hair is spread out around her head in a halo.

I watch her for as long as I can but I know I need to pee again so I drag myself out of bed and fight my way into the bathroom. The vanity mirror is large and tilted down and I blink sleepily at my reflection. I can see the full horrifying extent of the wrinkles in my clothes as well as the creases on my face. After Becca wakes up we need to get some coffee. I use the bathroom then splash water on my face and through my hair with my fingers.

When I come back into the room she's sitting up on the bed wearing jersey pajamas with cartoon cats on them. For a quick flash of a moment it feels like we're a couple on a vacation together, maybe even a honeymoon.

"Want to go check out the hotel breakfast?" I say.

"Sure." She takes some clothes from her backpack and takes a turn in the bathroom. I decide this is a good time to press my pants and shirt so I don't look quite as rumpled going out in public. I open the closet and see the iron up on the top shelf. But the cord is hanging down so I take hold of that and yank the iron down onto my lap. Victory.

I lay the ironing board across my lap and bring it over to the bed. Then I start with taking off my shirt since that's easiest.

I didn't expect how fast Becca gets ready. I've never seen a girl come out of the bathroom as quickly as she does. Even before my accident I would take longer than she just did. I'm still sitting in just slacks while I iron my shirt.

"Oh!" She says seeing me half naked. To be honest I think my chest is looking pretty good and my shoulders and arms have become more muscular than they've ever been. But my lower ab muscles are paralyzed so my belly sticks out. The shape of my body has changed considerably since the accident.

"Sorry," I say, "I just wanted to get some of the wrinkles out." I unplug the iron and hurry back into my shirt. The pants will have to wait. I almost look presentable.

Together we find our way to the continental breakfast where we see Becca's parents are already sitting at a table and several other people greet Becca as we pass. Becca confidently leads us straight to her parents' table and says, "You wait here, Jack. I'll go get us food. What do you like?"

"Could you find some black coffee for me? That and a piece of toast will be perfect."

She nods and then leaves me sitting with Mr. and Mrs. Cohen. Awkward.

"So, Jack, what do you do?" Mrs. Cohen asks.

"I'm in banking. I manage portfolios for Fortune 500 companies."

I wait for them to look impressed and make approving noises but Mr. Cohen says, "From a wheelchair?"

"The chair is a new addition to my accessories," I say. "But so far I'm not finding that it holds me back in the finance sector."

"Fair enough," he says.

Thankfully Becca comes back quickly and I gulp down coffee from a styrofoam cup.

We all eat and talk while interrupted every minutes by people stopping by to congratulate the parents of the bride.

When Becca and I are alone at the table together at last I say, “Maybe it would be best if I didn’t go to the actual wedding? Since I wasn’t invited?”

Her face falls. “You’ve come this far. It will be very helpful for me to have you there.”

“If you’re sure it’s okay,” I say.

“I’m supposed to go over and get my hair and makeup done in a little bit.”

"Okay you go see your sister. I need to find a suit."

"You'll be okay on your own?"

"I will." In fact, this trip has gone a long way to prove to myself that I’m resourceful and creative and I can handle the challenges that come up.

It’s not just a suit either. I’m going to need more catheters, a razer, a toothbrush, and a few other things. And I should probably ask Dr. Wilson to call in some emergency prescriptions. Then again we’ll be flying back tomorrow so maybe I can just wait.

Becca

I'm nervous about finding my way to the room where the bridesmaids are getting ready so I'm glad to see my cousin Lauren and I tag along with her. When I get there Leah is sitting in a chair with her makeup all done and her hair in progress. My veil is on a table beside her.

She looks odd because she's wearing jeans and a tank top with intense wedding makeup and hair on top.

When she sees me her eyes narrow. "Mom told me about your friend," she says. "I knew you were going to do this."

"Oh good. If you already knew then there's no issue." How she knew I was going to bring Jack when I didn't know myself is a mystery but I can't pretend to know what goes on in my sister's head.

"No, I mean I knew you would find a way to make it about you. It's supposed to be my day and now you've brought a man in a wheelchair to take all the attention. You always do this to me."

The other bridesmaids try to look busy with other things.

I don't know what to say. I just wanted Jack with me and the fact he's in a wheelchair wasn't a consideration. I don't think I even would have made it to the wedding if not for his help and support. I didn't intend to draw any attention. It's not my fault that disability makes people curious.

"Just once," Leah says quietly, "I want the focus to be on me. This should have been my time."

"It is!" I say. "This is your day and everyone is here to see you. I didn't mean to cause any issues."

"You never do, do you? You never intend harm and yet it follows in your wake while you're blissfully unaware."

Is that true? If I'm unaware, what can I do to fix it? How can I be any different from how I am? I've spent most of my life trying to improve myself, trying to fix my issues. Has none of that helped?

The panic is rising in me but I cannot melt down here. That will make things so much worse. By my side I'm flicking my fingers over and over trying to release stress like a steam valve.

Leah shakes her head and turns her attention back to the mirror and her hairdresser. "Just go," she says and it's clear she's talking to me even though she's not looking at me. I dare not ask about my hair.

When I get back to the room Jack is still out shopping. I get changed into my navy blue bridesmaid dress and try to do something nice with my hair.

Jack returns with shopping bags hanging from the back of his chair. He has figured out that he can wedge the door open, then grab hold of the door frame and yank his wheelchair through. After he gets through the door he looks up and stops short.

"That dress looks amazing on you," he says.

I smile. "Thank you."

"Okay, I need to get caught up. What time is the first event?"

"The ketubah signing and bedeken are next but that's just for the immediate family."

"What do those words mean?"

At this point he must know that asking me questions is going to result in having his ears talked off. I have to conclude that he enjoys it. "The ketubah is the wedding contract. It's a beautifully calligraphed and decorated page that most couples hang up in their homes. Part of it includes the tradition of bedeken where the groom lifts up the veil to make sure he has the right bride. It comes from the Bible story where Jacob is tricked into marrying the older sister of the woman he actually wanted. And you know what's funny?"

"What?"

"The wrong bride was named Leah. So it's kind of ironic in this case that the correct bride is Leah."

Jack laughs. "That is indeed ironic. So while you're at those ceremonies I can use the room to get changed?"

"That will be perfect. I'll knock before I come back in." Just saying that has me unintentionally thinking about what he looks like naked. I saw him shirtless this morning and the urge to run my fingers over his smooth skin was intense. I imagine undressing him and my body tingles. I chastise myself and hurry from the room.

At the ketubah signing I try to fade into the background of the room as much as possible. I don't want to do anything to set Leah off again. She enters the room looking stunning in a simple white dress with my knit lace veil covering her head and face.

I hope she understands that the veil is a gesture of care and love. I don't want our relationship to be strained but it never seems like anything I try heals the gap between us.

Larry lifts the front of the veil up and I smile to see how much love is in his face as he looks at my sister.

The signing is a brief ceremony so I'm back to the room pretty quickly. I knock and I hear Jack tell me to come in. I open the door and my knees go weak when I see him.

If he thought I looked good it's nothing compared to how great he looks. His suit is a deep midnight blue with a sheen like you're staring into the night sky. It perfectly follows his lean form. A crisp white shirt peeks out beneath the jacket and a rich burgundy tie's knot shows between the sharp v-points of his collar. One button of his jacket is buttoned and the second is unbuttoned, the edges of the jacket opening out onto the seat of the wheelchair. The pants are a perfect color match to the jacket and they go long enough that even sitting down they half cover his shining black shoes. No tie around his ankles this time.

I realize I'm staring and maybe even slobbering a bit. This man is far too good-looking for me.

He grins. "You like it?"

"I don't even know how you managed to find a custom-tailored suit in a strange city with no warning. That must be some kind of superpower."

"It is," he says. "Shall we?" He gestures to the door. I hold it open and he once again puts his fingers on the outside edges of the doorframe and pulls himself through.

The ceremony is in a grassy field. A chuppah has been erected and lines of folding chairs are set up.

Since I'm in the wedding party I say goodbye to Jack and go to line up for the walk down the aisle.

The music starts and we process. Despite what Leah thinks I really don't like being the center of attention. I'm holding a bouquet so that stops me from fidgeting with my hands. Normally if I were walking down an aisle with a bunch of people watching me I'd be flicking my fingers.

I focus on looking at the flowers. They are a stunning collection of calla lilies, roses, baby's breath and hydrangeas. Cool thing about hydrangeas is that their colors are determined by the Ph levels of the soil they grow in.

At the edge of the chuppah I stop and turn, watching as Larry is escorted down the aisle by his parents and then everyone stands and watches as Leah walks down the aisle with our parents on either side of her.

Even though Leah is frequently upset with me she is still my sister and I think I still love her. Love has always been a difficult topic for me. I tell my family I love them because I know it would upset them if I admitted that I'm not really sure what love feels like but I assume I have it. It's hard for me to be deceptive but not impossible. In this case the deception protects them. Besides, I am sure I must love them. I just don't know how to identify that emotion.

The point is that it's really special getting to see her get married. I'm standing very close to the action and I can see the way she and Larry look at each other. It's lovely. Her nose is turning red as she tears up.

As they say their vows I glance at Jack who is sitting in the back behind the rows of folding chairs in the grass. He is looking at me too and his face is impenetrable. I wonder what he's thinking but I can't ask so I turn my attention back to my sister.

The glass is brought out in a satin bag and placed at Larry's feet. He stomps hard on the bag and we all hear the glass shattering. "Mazel Tov!" the crowd shouts. I look at Jack again and I might be imagining it but I think he's sad. Is it strange for him to see Larry stomp on the glass knowing that he can't do that himself?

Paul's name tag is next to mine at the reception table. Of course there's no planned spot for Jack and the catering staff is trying to squeeze another place setting in. The width of his chair is more than the fancy reception chairs but I don't dare suggest he transfer out of his wheelchair because I know he hasn't been practicing that skill. I have the staff set him up next to me and gently push Paul further out so when it comes time for dinner Jack is on my right side and Paul is to his right.

However, Paul doesn't let this dissuade him at all. He just talks right past Jack as though he's not there. Next to Jack's immaculate suit, Paul's looks like he pulled it out of a dumpster. He's getting butter on the cuffs of his sleeves as he leans over and tells me all the specs of a new fast train that's being built to go between Boston and Florida.

I notice Jack finishing his first glass of wine before the salad course is done.

I must admit that Leah was not wrong about Jack attracting attention. Not only is he the only person in a wheelchair, he also looks incredibly slick. Every detail of his appearance is polished to perfection. People are looking and people are whispering. All the guests are trying to figure out who he is. He's also the least Jewish looking person in the room.

Paul eventually gets up to dance when the horah starts and Jack and I are alone at the table.

"You like that guy?" Jack asks, eyeing me closely. I duck my head and my curls fall across my eyes.

"No," I say. "He's an ass."

Jack laughs and I have to smile back. I am aching to say more, to tell him the truth. To tell Jack that he is the one I want to be with, that I daydream about him kissing me, that I want to shove him against the wall and climb onto his lap and ravage his beautiful lips. Instead I sip my water.

"Did your sister like the veil?" Jack asks. I look at his long fingers as they graze the gleaming silver fork.

"She was too busy being angry at me for showing up with a plus one."

"Isn't that odd? Wouldn't you be expected to bring a plus one?"

"Ha. I don't think my family will ever not see me as a child. Besides my mom doesn't want me bringing a date, she wants me to marry Paul."

Jack raises an eyebrow and says in a low voice, "Am I a date?"

What can I say to that? How much I want to say yes, how much I want to ask him if that's okay with him. But everyone I know doesn't think Jack could possibly like me, even Sam. She is the most polite about discouraging me but there's no doubt that she is skeptical about my crush. Even I am skeptical about my crush. I'm not the kind of woman this handsome and successful man wants on his arm.

For a moment I pause and think about the phrase "on his arm" and how it might no longer work for Jack now that he can't stand. What is the equivalent for a paraplegic? Well, regardless I am not the kind of woman that belongs with someone like him. I accepted that a long time ago, didn't I?

Would it hurt to ask him? To find out if my assessment is correct? I try to imagine saying the words to him right now. It could hurt. It could hurt a lot. I can already feel my heart sinking in pain as I think about how he would look at me, how he would let me down gently.

Then I realize I never answered his question and he's still looking at me with what might be amusement playing around his lips. He swirls the wine in his glass.

I'm stuck. I can't speak. The effort of pushing words through my body, past my voice box, is far too difficult. I just stare at him, mouth agape.

That's when the DJ announces the bouquet toss and before I know it my mother is there, pushing me out of my seat and towards the dance floor. I look back at Jack but his face is unreadable, at least to me.

I have zero interest in making a fool of myself jumping to catch the flowers. The whole ritual is just ridiculous.

I'm pushed into a small crowd of female relatives and as a group I think we resemble a compost heap after someone mowed wildflowers.

The bouquet arcs into the air. All eyes in the room follow it. My young cousins jump but it soars above their fingertips. And then it starts down and lands squarely on Jack's lap. There's dead silence for seconds. Leah turns around to see who caught it and her smile freezes on her face.

Despite high heels she stomps over to us, snatches the flowers back and hurls them to the floor.

"You," she points her finger at me. Everyone in the room is staring at her in stunned silence. "I am so sick of your antics, Becca. You might have everyone else wrapped around your finger but you're not fooling me."

Probably not the best time to be trying to visualize how people would get themselves wrapped around one of my fingers.

"Who is this guy?"

"This is my friend Jack."

"You trying to take advantage of her trusting nature or what?" she says to him directly.

Jack puts up his hands like he's surrendering. "She needed some support to make it here and I helped out, nothing untoward is happening."

Even though I definitely wish it would.

"She's a user, Jack. She latches onto people, gets all adorable and vulnerable, and squeezes them dry."

"Despite appearances, I can take care of myself, thanks."

“Both of you get out,” she says pointing to the exit of the reception hall.

“Come on, Becca,” Jack says quietly, “Let’s give her some space.”

I don’t want to, I want to resolve things right now. I hate leaving things, especially when I feel misunderstood. But Jack is right, there’s no reasoning with Leah right now. I follow him out.

We end up sitting on a park bench in our evening wear. At least I’m sitting on the bench and Jack is sitting beside it.

"Maybe I need to post this on Reddit AITA threads," I suggest.

"Post it where?"

"You know, Am I The Asshole. Where you tell your side of the story and the Internet judges if you're in the right or not. I can't rely on my own judgment so it helps to have strangers weigh in."

"You have me. You don't need strangers on the Internet who don't see the whole context. You are not an asshole.”

Then he surprises me by saying, “But I can see why Leah is frustrated with you."

"You can? Please tell me. I've been trying to figure it out for years."

"Let me see if I can put into words what I'm seeing. I don't know if you see yourself as a special needs person but your parents have definitely seen you as a special needs child. It can be hard on siblings when they have a brother or sister with challenges. So much attention and care goes towards that child and it can build up resentment."

I consider that. In my mind I play back every interaction with my sister I can remember since our earliest childhood. I think Jack is onto something.

“What should I do? I don’t want to be upsetting her all the time.”

"I think you should apologize to her. Sincerely. I know from your perspective you haven't done anything that warrants an apology but I think it will really help if you let her feel heard and seen."

I don't see how an apology is going to heal years of misunderstanding and mistrust but I'm willing to try anything.

When we get back to the hotel Leah is slouched on a sofa in the lounge area still in her wedding dress.

"You ruined my wedding, you self-absorbed bitch."

"All I did was show up, you're the one who attacked me in the middle of your own reception. How is it always my fault?"

"You push me to my breaking point every time and I know you're doing it on purpose."

"Why would I do that on purpose? What benefit could that possibly be to me?"

We're falling into old patterns and escalating but Jack takes my hand and gives a gentle squeeze reminding me that I'm supposed to be apologizing.

"Listen, Leah. I'm sorry. Truly I am. I haven't been at all mindful of your feelings over the years and I've made excuses for it. I should have noticed how you were being neglected and I'm so sorry that it's taken me this long to realize. Please let me make it up to you."

She stares at me in silence. All the fight has gone out of her eyes. Then she looks to my side and says, "Is this your doing?"

Jack answers, “It’s Becca’s real feelings, I just helped her put them into words. She loves you and she never meant to hurt you.”

Leah accepts that answer. Our relationship isn’t magically fixed but it feels like we’re in a much better place than it’s ever been. And even though I do get a lecture later from Mom, it’s not as brutal as I expected

Jack and I return to our room and I thank him for all he’s done to help. That’s when I notice that he’s gritting his teeth and small nerve spasms are twitching down his legs. He holds tight to the wheelchair armrests.

“Are you okay?”

“I left my anti-spasm medication at Thatcher,” he says.

Oh no. Something else that’s all my fault. I dragged him along and made him come with me even though he didn’t have the things he needed.

“I’m sorry,” I say, stricken.

“I’m okay. Let’s just get to bed."

Jack

By the time we're flying home I feel like a new man.

Now that I've been out in the real world I can see Becca's point that it's not a bad thing to learn wheelchair skills while still working at healing. She spots for me as I make the transfer to the airplane seat. Becca climbs over me to her seat. I push mine back and groan, closing my eyes.

"Are you okay?" Becca asks.

"I think it's time for me to order my wheelchair," I say with a sigh. "My back is killing me."

She doesn't say I told you so but I can see it in her eyes. She can't hide her thoughts in the slightest. I chuckle and squeeze her hand. Then I let go so I can try to use both my hands to shift in the airplane seat. It's impossible to find a comfortable position. I try moving the seat back a little bit to lessen the pressure on my spine. A lightning bolt of pain shoots up my back and throws me sideways but the seat belt catches me.

My eyes are closed again and I'm surprised when I feel small hands stroking from my shoulders down my back. I relax into Becca's gentle massage.

"Sir, we need you to raise your seat to a full upright position for takeoff."

Of course. I push the little metal button in but the seat doesn't come up. Becca sees the trouble right away and helps lift the seat up for me. The flight attendant moves on down the aisle and then Becca continues to rub my shoulders.

"Thank you," I say. "That feels really good."

"I'm glad," she says with a smile. “I think you’re going to like having a real wheelchair. And just think, you’ll be the most recognizable person at the bank. Everyone will know they need the guy in the wheelchair."

"That's kind of horrifying," I say. She's not wrong, though. It would be good for me to look for the positives since I'm stuck in this situation.

"I'm sorry," she says. "I shouldn't have said anything."

I see the shadow of our previous fight pass over her face. "No, you're right," I say. Something in me has shifted and I can't explain it but for the first time I can visualize my life from where I'm at now. I still believe I'll walk again one day but I'm ready to make the best of life with paralysis until then.

I'm seeing Becca in a new light too after being around her family and seeing their dynamic.

"Seems like your family puts a lot of pressure on you," I comment.

"Do you think so? I always thought it was the normal amount. Does yours not put pressure on you?"

"I suppose they do, but it's different."

"How?"

How can I put into words what I observed in the way Becca's family treated her? It's like they only see her weaknesses. I've watched her refuse to accept limits and push to be the best version of herself she can be. I've seen her passion and dedication to learning. I've enjoyed the unique spin she has on what she sees in the world. I see so many strengths in her that they are blind to, it seems.

Finally I say, "I'm not sure they've noticed that you've grown up."

She smiles but sighs at the same time. "You're definitely right about that. I often wonder if there's anything I can accomplish that will actually make them proud. I'm not sure Leah even believes I have a disability. To her I'm just annoying and spoiled."

"You are most definitely not spoiled. I say as someone who was."

That makes her laugh.

The plane dips and Becca grabs tight hold of my hand. If this were any other situation I would kiss her right now. But I'm not sure of the ethics of kissing an autistic woman and I no longer know how to gauge if she's even interested. I never doubted my charm and good looks before. Yes, I'm arrogant. I've earned it. But now that confidence is gone.

The moment passes and not long after we're arriving back at Logan. I make Becca assure me that she is okay getting home and then I call up the same cab company again.

When I get back to Thatcher I see police cars parked out front. At first it doesn't occur to me that they are there because of me. Then I see my mother in the lobby and I've never seen her in such disarray. My father is there too talking with a police officer.

"What is going on?" I ask.

"Jack! Oh my God, you had us so worried. No one knew where you were." My mother runs over as best she can in stilettos.

My father sighs and rolls his eyes, clearly annoyed that it was all proven to be an overreaction. I see him reassuring the police officers that I'm not missing and nothing is wrong. They nod and head out.

Just as I was telling Becca that her family treats her like a child, I'm stunned to discover that mine has started to do the same. Yes, I saw I had missed calls from them over the weekend but I figured I would touch base when I got back. I had no idea they were out here thinking I died in a ditch somewhere.

"Mom, this is ridiculous. I'm a thirty-six year old man." And I've been operating independently for years. I know what's changed but I don't want to say it. Now that I'm paralyzed from the waist down, my own mother doubts my competence. I need to set some boundaries with her before she starts completely babying me.

"You're you know, things are different," she stumbles over the words, trying to dance around saying the truth.

"How? How are things different? Say it."

I wait but she says nothing. It's dead quiet now, everyone nearby just looking at me and my mother. Since she's not saying it, I give her answer for her. "Now I'm weak and vulnerable and needy and *crippled*."

My mother gasps and before she even realizes what she's doing she slaps me across the face. "Don't you ever use that word," she hisses.

At that point my father finally decides he should do something and he ushers her away. "It's okay, Marilyn. We'll talk about it later." She leans into him crying. It doesn't surprise me that my father prioritizes helping my mother over me.

My cheek stings but I ignore it as I turn the wheelchair and push past a bunch of staff trying to pretend that they didn't see it.

Now that I've resolved to live my life fully as I am, things move quickly. Bill happily gets me working on transfers, wheelies, steep ramps, and all sorts of other wheelchair life skills. I get fitted and my new chair turns up looking sharp. It's deep black all over and I think it looks great with my shoes. It's so lightweight and maneuverable and I can't even believe the difference from what I've been using up til now.

"Look at you!" Becca cries out when I turn up after therapy with black slacks and a white button-down shirt. She claps in delight and I do a few spins to show off.

"Guess where I'm off to," I say.

"I'm terrible at guessing games," she says.

"I'm going to hockey practice."

"Dressed like that?"

"I'll change first but then after that I'm going to hockey practice. I hope they'll have me."

"I'm sure they will. Have fun."

There's a bit of awkwardness between us now. I think we both sense that my time in Cedar Harbor is wrapping up. Real life is looming. I'm mostly ready for that change. I just wish I could take Becca with me. She's been a light in the darkness of my time here. I suppose she's been that for many of the people who have to transform their lives at Thatcher. I'm not special and I don't have any unique claim on her affection.

I change into the closest thing I have to workout clothes and take my new chair over to the ice rink. It's about a mile from Thatcher, maybe a little less, but the weather is getting warmer by the day and it's a beautiful stroll.

I make my way through the main gym to the back and push through to the ice rink area. The smacks of sticks on pucks echoes in the mostly empty rink. Every grunt, shout, and score is amplified by the high ceilings.

At the edge I lean my chin on my arms and look at the four guys shooting pucks back and forth, each of them strapped to a sled with a blade along the bottom. A few minutes later they notice me.

Murph is the first to slice to a stop next to me at the entrance to the ice. He pulls off his helmet and smiles. "Welcome back."

"Sweet ride, man," Robbie says with a grin.

"Ready to give hockey a try?" Murph asks.

"Let's do it," I answer with more confidence than I actually feel.

"Danny, will you get him a sled?" Murph says. To me he adds, "Daniel is our official 'closest to able-bodied person.'"

Dan rolls his eyes and mutters, "The things I put up with from you guys." But he pushes back off with the sharp ends of his short hockey sticks and I watch as he gets out of the sled on the other side of the rink.

While it's clearly an effort for him, he is standing. He holds onto the edge of the rink and makes his way towards a pile of supplies. His legs are spasming but he seems to be using the shaking to hold his weight just enough to keep him upright.

"How is he doing that?" I say before I can stop myself.

"Incomplete injury," Murph says.

Robbie elaborates. "With spinal cord injuries a lot comes down to how complete the injury is and the location on the spine." He shakily extends one of his arms and I see that his wrist is limp and his fingers stick together. "I've got a higher level injury than you or Dan. My spine is broken at a C level. Yours is probably a T level."

I nod. The doctor definitely said T-10.

Robbie continues, "Dan has a T level injury but the damage to his spine didn't destroy all the nerves so he has more function. Welcome to the kind of conversations you have after sustaining an SCI." He chuckles.

By this time Dan has sled back over pulling another sled behind him. "That and plenty of discussion of bowel programs," he says.

"As the only one here without paralysis, can I request a moratorium on the bowel talk?" Murph says but he's smiling.

The final man has been quiet so far. When I look more closely I see that he's actually very young, probably just a teenager. I look at his hands to see if I can apply what Rob has been telling me. The kid has his hockey sticks taped to his arms as Rob does but he also has a very high back on the sled. It appears to my untrained eye that he is the most severely disabled of us all.

"Dan and I will help you get into the sled," Murph says. "Are you able to safely get to the ground?"

I nod. This is one of my brand new skills, in fact. I try not to be thrown off my game by everyone watching me do it, though. I try to imagine it's just Bill watching. I set the brake on my chair, use my hands to scoot my butt forward to the front edge of the seat, hold onto the back with one hand and lean forward over my knees. I place my other hand flat on the floor and slowly tip the balance of my weight until I can bring my body fully to the ground.

I've totally got this.

Murph and Danny help guide me into the sled and strap me in. Then everyone gathers around and I'm handed a helmet, chest plate, and two small hockey sticks with picks on the other end. I feel ridiculous but I guess I'm ready for sport.

The guys show me how to push the sticks against the ice to move, how to pass the puck while sitting, and they tell me about the rules of hockey. It takes a few minutes to find my center of gravity and stay balanced but as I get the hang of it shooting across the ice in a giant skate is quite fun.

Becca

I've started a new knitting project and picked up some extra hours at work and the distractions are nice but there's still a feeling niggling at me and I don't know what it is but I don't like it. Jack has left Thatcher so it feels different when I'm over there volunteering. It was really nice having him with me for Leah's wedding. I'll always be grateful for that.

Sam comes over to watch The Bachelor with me one evening and I tell her, "I'm feeling something."

She looks at me with her full attention. "Good or bad?"

"Bad. I don't like it."

She thinks for a little while and then says, "Might I suggest that it could be heartbreak?"

I test that idea in my body and she might be right. I miss Jack. There's no doubt of that. Once again I wish I were someone different. I wish I was an elegant woman with style and grace. I imagine being a glittering socialite who holds court at the fanciest parties and everyone admires my charm and charisma. Jack is there, proud to be my man.

In all my years of self improvement I've never come even close to that vision. I could keep trying. Maybe one day years from now I can show up in Jack's world and amaze him with my transformation into just the right kind of woman for him.

The pain is squeezing in my chest.

"Oh sweetie," Sam says. She holds out her arms and I slip into her hug, tears leaking from my eyes onto her shirt.

"Jack must be a very special guy," Sam says.

After Sam goes home I know that one thing I need to do is break things off with Paul once and for all. Even if I never see Jack again, just knowing there's someone of his caliber out there I could never be content with Paul. He'll be the right match for someone else, I'm sure of it.

When I tell Paul that I don't want to be in a relationship with him he just says, "Your loss. But that playboy you're hanging out with is never going to understand you."

I don't think Paul understands me any better, even if we are both autistic.

Jack

"You've made so much progress, Jack," Dr. Wilson says, pumping my hand with hers. "Remember to sign up for the hand control driving class next month, okay? We'll see you then."

I'm getting back to my life and making the best of it.

My parents haven't reached out since the incident outside the rehab center. I think my mom is embarrassed about it and she can't face me.

I return to my condo and it feels odd. I've had to make arrangements to renovate and make all of it accessible. I never even thought before about things like making the bathroom doorway wider and replacing the claw foot tub with a roll-in shower. That one stings.

But it's also unnervingly quiet. Over the last several months I haven't been alone at all.

I look in my full length mirror and say out loud, "I am disabled." I pause and then keep going. Over and over I say, "I have a disability. I am a paraplegic." I keep saying these phrases waiting for them to feel real. What was it that therapist was saying about disabled identity? It's an identity that is added to other identities. Nothing needs to be lost.

Maybe I should call my mother and smooth things over but I don't feel up for whatever tactic she's going to use to make herself right. Instead I call my friend Margaret. We met a couple years ago at a charity gala and even though she's older than my parents, we hit it off.

"Where have you been?" Margaret's voice over the phone is surprisingly soothing in its familiarity.

I don't know how to answer that. Every sentence I start I can't figure out how to finish. There's so much and I don't know where to even begin.

"Well," I start. "Something happened."

"What is it?" The concern in her voice is barely perceptible. She's classic old money Boston but I've known her long enough to be able to read the subtle clues of her emotions.

"It's ironic, really," I say. "You and I have raised so much money for spinal cord injury research and now I'm the charity case."

"What?"

"I was in an accident in December. Now I'm the one who needs a wheelchair."

"My God."

I'm realizing that I'm going to spend the rest of my life giving the quick explanation of my disability. I will have to say, "Car accident" possibly every day. I wish I didn't have to think about getting hit by a truck every time a friend or stranger asks why I'm in a wheelchair.

"Meet me for lunch at the club tomorrow," she says.

"Will do." We hang up. It feels like pulling a bandaid off. But I have more people I'll have to tell.

That night I feel brutally lonely. I go through my evening routine as I learned it in rehab and it feels weird to be bringing that back with me into regular life. But of course this is my regular life now. Becca is right. Using the wheelchair isn't giving up, it's how I'm able to keep engaging in life.

I decide to go out and I call Hunter and Brooks to meet up for dinner at my favorite place in Harvard Square.

"Absolutely," Hunter says. "I'll be there."

"Sounds great," Brooks says.

I should probably call ahead and make sure it's accessible but I don't. What's the worst that could happen? We'll just go somewhere else if I can't get in.

It's close enough I don't need to get a ride. I wheel down the sidewalks. The curb cuts are hit or miss so I'm glad I learned to pop wheelies over curbs. It seems that the team at Thatcher does actually know what skills are important for me to know. The air is warm and a light breeze carries the scent of beer batter and brick.

My friends are waiting outside for me. As I approach Hunter says, "Wow. This is like, a thing now."

"Yeah," I answer. "For the foreseeable future I'll be turning up in a chair. Go ahead, ask me questions. Get it out of your system."

Not surprisingly Hunter starts and peppers me with a wide range of questions from how do I pee to how far out we are from a cure for SCI.

Brooks has different kinds of questions. He wants to know if I've tried meditation, yoga, or herbs. We did actually have a meditation teacher who would visit rehab. I don't think I would get very far with yoga.

The three of us head inside and have a nice time.

Hunter fills us in on his wife and kids. Brooks tells us about the guy he's just started seeing. I don't say anything about Becca but I'm definitely trying to picture how it would go if I was dating her. I think my friends would accept her, actually. They're taking this change with me better than I expected. It was awkward at first but we're finding our rhythm again.

There's only one club when Margaret says it. I have to take a cab there but as I pass by my car on the street I think *soon*. Soon I'll get the hand controls put on and learn to drive as a paraplegic. I've gotten much smoother at getting in and out of cabs. I'm an expert wheeler now.

The custom sized wheelchair is far easier to use but my time in the bulky one certainly built up my arm muscles. I've always been lean but now my dinner jacket is tight against my shoulders and biceps.

When I arrive at the Pinecrest Country Club I go straight to the dining room and Margaret is already there sitting at a table. She's an incredibly elegant woman. The kind of person who makes you want to sit up straighter whenever you're around her. She sees me and rises to her feet in a fluid motion and when I reach the table she puts a hand on my shoulder and leans down to kiss my cheek.

She sits back down and I start trying to pull one of the chairs away from the table to make room for my wheelchair. Margaret signals a waiter who rushes over to remove the chair for me.

"Jack, darling, this is certainly a surprise."

I chuckle and say, "It was a surprise for me too."

"I can imagine." She sips a glass of white wine. "What's the prognosis? Will you be able to recover eventually?"

I admit to myself at the same time that I tell her, "Probably not. It seems likely that I'll never walk again."

Margaret nods. "That's difficult to hear, I'm sure."

"That's an understatement."

The waiter returns and I ask for red wine and an avocado club sandwich. Margaret orders a spring salad.

"How is your work taking it?" Margaret asks.

"I've been working from the hospital but I haven't been back in person yet. Not sure what they'll think."

A group of golfers spills into the dining room from the green. I can feel their eyes on me as they gather around a table on the other side of the room.

"There's a fundraising ball coming up," Margaret says. "To benefit childhood cancer research. Would you like an invite?"

I used to go to events like this at least once a month. I try to imagine myself there. As Becca said, I just have to be confident and lean into being super visible as the guy in the wheelchair. No one can forget me and I can use that to my advantage in some ways. And I know how to project confidence even when I'm not feeling it.

"I would love to," I say.

Margaret holds out her glass and I clink mine with hers. "Cheers," she says.

Thinking of Becca and her unique take on things makes me a little sad. I do miss her. But in the world of schmoozing where what is unsaid matters more than what is said, it just feels cruel to bring an autistic woman into that. Then again I haven't even given her a chance to see how she likes it and I would be close by to protect her from backstabbing. It would be fun to see her take on everything.

"I'm going to powder my nose," Margaret says. She rises from the table and drifts from the room. Then another couple arrives for lunch and to my shock it's my parents. This is starting to feel like a set up.

I can't read the expression on my mother's botox-frozen face. My father looks as stern as he always does but that's not a real indication of his mood.

"Hello, Jack," my mother says as they arrive at my table.

I admit it feels weird to be sitting while they stand. Usually I would rise to greet them and as a fairly tall fellow it feels very strange to be looking up at them. My dad firmly shakes my hand but he glances down at the perfectly-fitting sleek black wheelchair and the corner of his lips tightens. I know he sees it as a sign I'm giving up on myself. I don't know how to explain to him that it's the opposite of that. I'm not completely giving up on the hope to walk again but I'm also going to be grateful for the second chance at life and live to the very fullest.

"How are you?" I ask them as they sit down.

"We've been well," my father says.

"How are you?" my mother adds.

"Still paralyzed," I say. I don't know why I want to needle her.

"Jack," my father chastises. "That's unkind."

"It's just a fact, Dad. You both have to get used to me being disabled. I've had to accept this reality and now it's your turn."

"So you're just going to stay stuck in that chair?" my father says.

"I'd be a lot more stuck if I didn't have it." How does he think I'm going to get anywhere without a wheelchair? I already tried willing my nerves to fix themselves and that was a total failure.

Margaret comes back to the table and I realize she's been standing to the side watching to see how this reunion goes. Time for her to intervene before another fight breaks out.

Her presence does cool things off and we have a stiff and pleasant lunch.

I'm glad after this to be going to hockey practice. Out in the world it feels like I have armor on. But when I get to the rink I'm surrounded by other disabled guys. Murph was right, he and the guys understand what I'm going through in a way that my friends and family never will.

"What, did you come from a funeral?" Danny says as I push my wheelchair into the ice rink area of the gym.

"Haha, very funny." These are the kind of guys who probably don't even own a suit. I could see Dan renting one if he needed one. But I wear them almost every day. I've even gotten the pants of all my suits tailored so they lay better when I'm sitting down. The guys can tease as much as they want, I know I look good.

"I'd love to see you play hockey in that," Danny says.

"I'm changing, just give me a minute."

"Or an hour," he says with a wink.

He's not exactly wrong. It does still take me a lot of time to change clothes. It's quite tough to take off and put on pants when you can't move your legs but I always get it eventually.

"Shut up," I say as I disappear through the locker room door.

When I come back out the others are already on the ice and my sled is waiting for me. I put the brakes on my wheelchair and maneuver my body down to the sled. Robbie holds the sled steady for me with his fist. Once I'm strapped in I realize that Robbie's girlfriend is here watching. She's Becca's best friend and I feel a pang in my chest when I see her.

After an invigorating hour of drills and skirmishes we come back off the ice and decide to go for drinks. There's a brewery nearby with a parking lot venue where you can mill around outside or sit at picnic tables enjoying the weather.

I get a beer even though I'm usually more of a wine guy and position my wheelchair beside a picnic table. Sam immediately sits down across from me and Robbie pulls up next to her.

"Is this an ambush?" I ask.

"Becca's been talking about you a lot," Sam says.

Dare I admit that I miss her? Without her, life is far more dull. I don't say anything. Sam continues, "I love her to pieces but I also know that for a lot of people she's an acquired taste. I wanted to get a sense from you whether you're interested or if she's off the mark. You know what I mean?"

Acquired taste is an interesting way to put it. I can't say I feel that way about Becca at all. I found her fun to be around from the moment she explained that first joke to me. Nearly every interaction I've had with her has made me lighter and happier.

Finally I say, "I think she's too good for me."

Sam and Robbie exchange a look.

"So you do like her?" Sam says.

"Of course I do but what do I even have to offer her anyway?"

"You can offer her you," Sam says emphatically

"Can I level with you?" Rob says.

"Okay..."

"What Becca needs is someone who listens to her, someone who believes in her abilities, someone who doesn't make her feel like a freak. Isn't that right, Sam?"

"Yes. Couldn't have said it better. And I think from what she's told me that you have those qualities."

"I don't think she's interested in me like that anyway."

Sam snorts. "I can assure you that she is. She sucks at identifying her emotions but I'm telling you she is head over heels in love with you."

"Can I ask an insensitive question?" I say.

"Shoot," Sam says.

"I don't know anything about autism. Are there any ethical issues with me asking her out on a date?"

"Ethical issues?"

"I'm not trying to be an asshole but I just don't know and I need to be sure I'm not being inappropriate."

"Oh, I get it," Robbie says. "No ethical issues as long as you listen to her. She's an adult and she can consent."

Sam nods enthusiastically. "Absolutely," she says. "Becca gets treated with kid gloves too much. She's a grown woman and she wants to be loved just like any other woman.

"In that case, there's a party I need to invite her to."

Becca

I can't even watch my favorite comedians and analyze how they've used misdirection in their jokes without thinking of Jack.

I thought I had been in love before but now I know that was nothing. The aching hole of him in my life is unlike anything else.

It's so stupid that I let this happen. What did I expect, that Jack was going to take me to charity balls and show me off to his friends and family? Me? Yeah right.

I need to get back to reality and move forward from this crush.

And then one day while I'm deep in coding I'm startled by my phone vibrating. When I look it's my sister. I have her number programed in because of family group texts but I don't think she's ever called me or texted just me. Is something wrong? Immediately I start to worry that Mom and Dad have been hurt.

I pick up the phone. "Hello?"

"Hi, Becca. It's Leah."

"I saw. Is everything okay?"

"Oh yeah. I just got back from my honeymoon and I thought maybe we could have lunch."

For several seconds I just sit there holding the phone and say nothing.

"Becca? Are you there?"

"Yes, I would love that."

"Great. Can I pick you up at your place tomorrow?"

Quickly I flip through a mental calendar. I'll have to tell Sam I won't be at the store but that's the only thing. "Sure," I say.

The next day Leah picks me up and we go to the Steamy Beans Cafe and Coffee Shop.

"I was surprised to hear from you," I say once we're seated with our bagels and lox. "I swear I really didn't mean to upstage you by bringing Jack along."

"I know," she says. "I've been giving it a lot of thought and I think it's time you and I started fresh as sisters. I've been holding onto stuff from the past and seeing you as you were years ago. I feel like I haven't even met the woman you are today."

Tears well up in my eyes. "I would love to get to know who you are too," I say.

She smiles. "Good. Now tell me, did you enjoy the wedding?"

"Other than the fight, yes. It was beautiful and I'm so happy for you. How was the honeymoon?"

"A marvelous reset." She leans forward conspiratorily. "What's going on with you and Jack? He seemed pretty smitten with you."

I sigh. "You know I'm not good at reading people and situations. I hoped he was smitten with me but I think I was wrong."

"You might be bad at reading people but I'm not. I have a feeling you'll be hearing from him."

As soon as she says it my phone starts to ring. I stare at it and back at Leah. "It's him," I say.

She laughs so hard other people turn to look at us. "Well, go on and answer it then," she says.

I pick up the phone and say, "Did Leah put you up to calling me?" Across the table Leah facepalms.

"No," Jack says. He sounds confused.

"Oh."

"I was calling because I got an invitation to a charity ball and I was hoping you might like to go with me. You can wear your bridesmaid dress."

"I won't fit in."

"Neither will I. Let's go be misfits together, okay?"

"That sounds nice," I say. He gives me the details and then we hang up.

"Well?" Leah says.

"He invited me to a ball."

"Knew it," she says and takes a bite of her bagel. "He's pretty yummy. Shame about the wheelchair."

I don't know what to say to that so I ignore it and think about what it will be like going to a fancy event.

The ball is exactly how I imagined it would be. Like Cinderella and Pride& Prejudice and Bridgerton. Beautiful people everywhere you look. Crystal chandeliers glittering far overhead. Enormous floral arrangements on every table. Waiters carrying around trays of hors d'oeuvres. My eyes must be as big as saucers.

A tray passes by with little bits of toast and cheese. I take a pat of cheese and pop it in my mouth. Oh dear. That wasn't cheese, it was butter. I look down at Jack and he's trying not to laugh.

"I would have warned you," he says, "But the waiter only lowered the tray for me to see after it was too late."

"This is a bad idea. I can't do this."

"Nonsense, you're doing great. And you look more beautiful than anyone here."

I smile. I am wearing the bridesmaid dress as he suggested. He's got an even more incredible suit on. This one is a light blue that somehow exactly matches the color of his eyes. I could really get lost in those eyes.

An older gentleman comes slowly over to us. It's hard to know if we just happened to cross paths or if he was aiming for Jack.

"Good to see you, my boy," he says.

I don't think that's Jack's dad, though. I'm pretty sure I saw his dad a couple times at Thatcher.

"Sir Edward, great to see you again. I'd like you to meet my date this evening, Miss Rebecca Cohen."

"A pleasure," the old man says with a happy smile.

This is a good time to practice the small talk I've been working on with Sam. The flower arrangements on the table heavily feature sunflowers and so I say, "Did you know that sunflowers can absorb radioactive isotopes out of soil and help to clean up nuclear disasters? They are hyperaccumulating plants and they can bring contaminants into their stems and leaves and hold them there. They call it phytoremediation when they use plants to clean sites of environmental toxins."

"Well, isn't she illuminating?" Sir Edward says to Jack.

He grins. "She certainly is."

The gentleman moves along to greet someone else and I bite my lip and look to Jack.

"Was that a disaster? I probably embarrassed you."

But Jack smiles the widest I've ever seen and says, "That was perfect. I'm going to need you to stop talking like you're so beneath everyone else. You are important to this world. You, exactly as you are. You inspired me, you challenged me, you have touched me in a way no one else ever has. You have gifts and I love every single thing about you."

I stare at him. "You love me?"

"Can you think of any other reason I would haul my ass to Logan airport with almost no wheelchair practice? Because I can't."

Can I? I consider the possibilities. There must be other reasons than love.

“Don’t think about it too hard,” he says.

“Okay.”

"May I call you my girlfriend, Miss Rebecca Cohen?"

"Only if you kiss me right now."

"Deal."

He takes my hand in his and gently pulls me towards him. I wrap my other hand around the back of his neck and press my lips to his. There’s an instant burst of heat throughout my body and I groan. He switches his hands to my waist and pulls me right onto his lap. His lips are firm and soft, his breath warm. I rake my fingers through his short hair and his breath hitches. We can’t get close enough, each of us pressing against the other.

“Get a room, you two,” someone passing by says.

Jack pulls his lips back and whispers into my ear, “Good idea.”

The End

Thank you for reading! If you enjoyed this book I hope that you'll consider **leaving a review** wherever you purchased this book and/or Goodreads. It helps a lot :)

.

You can get bonus content at my website: www.RuthMadisonBooks.com!

www.ingramcontent.com/pod-product-compliance
Lightning Source LLC
La Vergne TN
LVHW020717110826
845149LV00012B/2300